GIMMICKS
AND GLAMOUR

Praise for *Boy at the Window*

"Ellzey's novel is a sensitive story from a gifted writer...
While the book has some triggering content, such as suicide
attempts and mental illness, the author never equates Daniel's
mental struggles to his sexuality. It is a very keen move to draw
that line very cleanly. Daniel is a fresh take on LGTBQIA+
youth representation who many readers will gravitate to; he
is relatable without being stereotypical and his story is one
young adults will want to read. VERDICT: This debut novel
belongs on the shelves of all libraries that serve high school
readers."—*Roy Jackson, School Library Journal*

"In his daydreams, Daniel, who is White and Korean, is the
confident leader of the Lost Boys who spends his days seeking
treasure and battling Captain Hook. There are no strict, distant
parents in Neverland, no homophobic classmates, no pressure
for him to be someone he isn't. In real life, Daniel is a junior
at Cranbrook Prep in Southern California, having transferred
to the school for a fresh start following a suicide attempt over
the summer...The portrayals of mental illness and trauma
recovery are handled honestly and sensitively. There is no
magical solution...An ultimately uplifting story that does not
shy away from the discomfort of reality."—*Kirkus Reviews*

"This book centers the experience of a queer and neurodiver-
gent Korean-American person, and the cast of side characters
is also quite diverse! Therapy is depicted in a very realistic way
and the relationship between the main character and therapy is

super relatable. In this book, you get both a YA contemporary romance and some extremely interesting fabulism elements. Mental health issues are shown as something that affect many of us and in vastly different ways, and safe spaces are depicted as essential and as something that might mean something completely different for each of us."—*ReadAndyRead*

"The story overall is interesting and engaging. The development of Daniel and his love interest Jiwon is compelling. I liked the way Ellzey explored their blossoming relationship to a slow burn as they sorted out their feelings for each other, their families, and their own identities."—*Punk Ass Book Jockey*

By the Author

Boy at the Window

Gimmicks and Glamour

Visit us at www.boldstrokesbooks.com

GIMMICKS
AND GLAMOUR

by

Lauren Melissa Ellzey

2023

Credits
Editor: Jenny Harmon
Production Design: Stacia Seaman
Cover Design by Inkspiral Design

GIMMICKS
AND GLAMOUR

CHAPTER ONE

H ow are you feeling today, Ashly?"
I stare the college guidance counselor down. Her
hair is pinned in an impeccable bun. Her lipstick is so neutral,
you'd think her face is au naturel. But there's nothing natural
about sitting with a practical stranger and being asked about
my life like it's a subject for small talk.

By now, I've figured out that when adults ask me how I'm
doing, there are only a few general replies that make the cut.
I'm good is the best. All the problems get buried under a sea of
good. *I'm happy!* warms hearts, because adults love happy kids
almost as much as they love obedience. *I'm hungry/thirsty* is
permitted, because those states of being are easy fixes. And
then there's the silent response. Silence is easy, because adults
can fill it in with *She's just shy*, or *She's doing well*, or *She's a
bit sleepy this morning.*

No one wants to hear *I'm angry.* Especially not my tennis
instructor meeting me for the first time, or my parents, when I
got off the middle school bus to join them on the porch, or my
aunt, come to visit over Christmas, or my therapist back in the
seventh grade. Well, at first my therapist liked hearing about
the angry feelings, but even she got tired of it after a couple
of weeks.

"Try not to hide your real feelings behind the anger," my
therapist said, and it was honestly reason enough for me to

never take her advice. I'm not hiding behind anger. I'm angry, and I mean it.

Today, I settle for "I could be better."

Mrs. Sherry shifts in her seat. "I imagine you know why you're here, then. It's about graduation. We want to help you get on the right track so you can get that diploma in June."

According to the local high school survival handbook, my entire life centers around a diploma. Beyond that, I'm best off taking my daily prescription of pretending. If I pretend to be straight, I'm better off than being bisexual. If I follow my peers' beauty standards, I can pretend that my naturally tan skin is the result of summer vacations, pretend that my curly hair doesn't exist, since it's hidden in the sulfur smell of Brazilian blowouts. I can act like my African American father is invisible if no one sees his photograph. And then everyone else can feel more comfortable when I'm standing in the middle of the Hackley High School hallway with the label *Straight White Girl* hanging over my head.

When I tried the *invisible* line on my dad, he told me to watch my mouth. Mom mentioned something about never making friends with an attitude like that. I shut it because a fight with them is never worth it. Sure, sneaking out is easy, but it's no fun being grounded for another month. Especially since, despite my attitude, I do have friends. Well, friend. Just one, but we'll get to her later. And the funny thing is, when you're pissed off all the time, no one at school hates you. I'd say they get a kick out of me getting kicked out of class. I got high-fived in the eighth grade for tagging the girls' restroom with a cursive letter to the principal: *Fuck off.* Not my most eloquent graffiti moment, but the high-five made the suspension worth it.

"Your parents are aware of the situation," Mrs. Sherry adds. "Together, we can come up with a plan to help you graduate on time."

It's not that I don't like my parents. I just don't think they knew what they signed up for when they decided to have a kid. I think they thought the worst of their troubles would be their interracial wedlock. But I guess a mixed baby is a mixed bag, and they're too heterosexual to realize that bisexuality doesn't die off with a first kiss from a boy. Nothing changed after I lost my virginity at age fifteen in the back seat of my boyfriend's dad's pickup truck. I broke up with him, by the way. Something about him deserving better and me just being bored of him.

Mrs. Sherry taps her manicured finger on the stack of papers on her desk. No doubt, it's my disreputable school record. "You'll need to make up the work you missed last semester," she says. "You're not in any clubs or on any sports teams. You've got time. Even though there's only one semester left, you can still pull yourself out of this."

What Mrs. Sherry doesn't know is that the only thing I've still got going for me is tennis. Thank God for private sports clubs, because I wouldn't make the disciplinary cut for any school team. And before you even ask, I don't play doubles anymore. It's me, my racket, and a ball to smash. Beyond that net, there may as well be a ball machine spitting at me. Breathe in, side shuffle, forward swing. Breathe out, backpedal, backhand. I love those tennis balls almost as much as I love Caris. But now isn't the time to be thinking of Caris. I need to get through this first day back from winter break. Caris isn't here anyway. She's miles away, so I'm stuck with a school full of loaded expectations, flimsy frenemies, and shadows. I might as well walk the halls alone.

❖

Once I'm freed of the guidance office, I head to the Student Union to pick my second semester schedule. I'm in line for all of two seconds when a teacher I don't even recognize tells me that my skirt is too short. I untuck the waistband without a word, because the moment she walks away, I'll tuck it back anyway. I've never understood the point of dress codes, and with just under six months left till the final high school bell of my life, I don't think now is the time for contemplating modesty or conformity.

At least I've got a tennis jacket on over my cropped polo shirt. Winter calls for layers, but it's San Diego, so what is winter anyway but an occasional stiff breeze and some gray days? I finally make it to the front of the line and mutter my last name. Most seniors have a free period for their last class, but since I failed art last semester, I've gotta take an extra elective. Hooray for seventh period choir. So long as I show up and open my mouth, I'll pass. I don't even have to actually sing.

On my way to my locker, Bradley Jameson saunters over with his lettermen crew. "Missed you at the New Year's party," he says with a crooked grin that's supposed to make me swoon. I wonder how his teeth stay so white when he's always the first to throw up after a round of Jell-O shots.

"I had other plans," I say. My fingers dial my locker combination code. I'm relieved when the lock pops open, because I was honestly just relying on muscle memory.

"Last I checked you were still single."

I glide my fingers along binders and books. After a second glance at my schedule, I see I've still got English for my first period, so I just grab a simple folder from my backpack and stuff everything else into my locker. We never use the English textbook anyway. I can just share with a classmate if Mr. Campbell decides to switch it up on us.

"You are still single, right?" Bradley asks, leaning against the locker beside me. His grin is turned up at full wattage, and I want to shatter it, but after staying up till three last night, I'm a little too tired to play devil right now.

"My relationship status has nothing to do with whether or not I show up at a party," I say.

"I texted you."

"My number changed."

"You little liar." Bradley's cronies are bumping shoulders just a few paces away, and they aren't out of earshot. At this point, he's only pushing the conversation to save face. A girl with silvery wings saunters down the hall, casting a glance our way, but decides that the drama isn't worth it.

"Maybe you should ask your girlfriend if my phone number changed," I say. Not that picture-perfect Jasmine Bennett would ever thumb me into her contacts list, but that's not the point I'm trying to make.

"We broke up right before Christmas. Artistic differences."

The closest Bradley's ever gotten to art is tracking mud on the bleachers after a football game. "Sorry to hear that, Brad. Not interested in a rebound."

His eyes dart nervously toward his friends. "That's not what you said last year."

I slam my locker door. "Look, I get it. You're lonely and horny and pathetically available, but I'm much more interested in English class than this conversation, which isn't saying a lot. So, go pant after someone else. I'm hoping to finish high school without having to endure your bad breath ever again."

The rest of the football team cracks up, and Brad turns a shade redder than my period blood. The bell rings. My work here is done.

I guess the devil in me can still come out to play after only three hours of sleep.

❖

Mr. Campbell has a new seating chart on the board, and sure enough, he's switched my seat to the back of the class. Guess that means he's given up on me, which is honestly the best news I've heard today. By some divine intervention, he's switched Caris's seat, too, but she's not here today, since her family decided to fly for a weeklong trip to Hawaii after New Year's Eve. Caris gets straight As, so I guess her parents figure a single day's extension of winter break won't set her back.

After I slide into my designated plastic chair, I grimace at the board for the last minute of the passing period. Sure enough, Mr. Campbell spelled my name incorrectly. *Ashley Harris*, it says. The usual error. There's the curly *e* that sneaks in before the *y*. Sometimes baristas get innovative with an *-ie* or *-eigh*. But no one thinks that maybe it's just an *L + Y* after Ash. Like an adverb. Like, "Hi, you can call me ashly."

Ashly, like what's left after a fire, but I'm always burning hot-coal bright. Like this Tyger in a poem we had to read in middle school. The poem was set *in the forests of the night*. When I read about the *Tyger Tyger burning bright*, I felt like, for once, I wasn't wasting time. To that long-dead poet, William Blake, and to whatever *immortal hand* of God you're hanging with in heaven by now, you got one thing right: *What the hammer? what the chain, in what furnace was thy brain?* If I could call up God and ask what furnace he forged me in and for what reason, I'm pretty sure he'd send me directly to voicemail. And nobody reads voicemail.

Once the bell rings, everyone settles into their new seats, and Mr. Campbell wastes no time before asking us for our winter break assignment. I'm still not sure how it's legal to close school for the holidays, and teachers are still allowed to assign essays.

I spent New Year's Eve with Caris, cranking out a final draft of a personal essay meant for the college applications I'm not planning to submit. Caris was flying out to Hawaii the next day, so it was New Year's Eve or never. With her help, my hot mess life transformed from that of an irascible she-tiger to a persevering tennis player. I typed up trash sentences. Caris edited with finesse. By the end of the night, buzzed on tiny bottles of dry red wine Caris had swiped, even I was starting to believe I had a tennis scholarship on the horizon. My backyard patio was magic, with Caris and me wrapped in fuzzy blankets and watching the stars that only I could see sailing around us. Then she went home right after midnight. I trudged past my snoring parents on the couch and curled into bed, trying to ignore the monsters in my closet. Still, a study night with Caris was better than getting drunk with Bradley, High School Extras, and Co.

Caris is destined for college, but she never talks about her applications, which is bizarre because she makes great grades. She could be in all advanced classes if she felt like it. Back in sophomore year I asked her why she was slumming it with me in Algebra 1 when she already knew calculus. She grinned and said, "Somebody's gotta keep you in line." It's the closest anyone's come to telling me they love me, besides my parents.

After I pass my essay forward, I bury my tired eyes into my white tennis jacket, only vaguely aware that I might smudge mascara on the sleeves. Caris's desk yawns emptily beside me. She'll be back tomorrow, and then I'll be more like myself. What's the point in being angry without a friend to egg you on and laugh in the aftermath. That's just lonely.

CHAPTER TWO

Caris's flight arrives at exactly 1:02 a.m. sharp. I know this because she tells me so when she shows up at my window one and a half hours later. Any normal person might be irritated to wake to someone tapping on their window when they had finally managed to wrestle themself to sleep on a school night, but I'm out of my bed like a bullet. After ten years of friendship, I can recognize Caris's shadow behind the glass.

I open the window, push out the half-detached screen, and fling myself out of the one-story house. Fingers of chilly night air grip my bare legs. I cross my arms over my threadbare T-shirt and wish that I'd slept in pants instead of pajama shorts.

"Get a phone already," I tell her for the thousandth time.

By now, my eyes have finally focused in the darkness. I glance around for any other visitors, but it's only Caris tonight. She grins, her teeth and eyes glinting in the lights cast from distant streetlamps.

"Talk to my parents about it," she says without a trace of annoyance.

Caris shattered her first cell phone the day her parents bought it for her thirteenth birthday. Believe it or not, they bought her a second one the very next day, and this klutz dropped it in the toilet hours later. Eventually, they gave up and just bought her a planner instead. To be honest, I don't blame them. After she destroyed four phones in a row, even I started to wonder if she was breaking them on purpose. Thing is, Caris isn't the clumsy type. She has this way of walking, talking, and breathing that floats like oil on water.

A breeze picks up, and I shiver. So, Caris takes off her buttonless jean jacket and tucks it over my shoulders. The pendant on her necklace swings against her throat. A Dara knot is etched onto the thin silver pendant. Overlapping lines weave together into a four-part hexagon. She wears the necklace every day, and it always makes me think of my grandma back in Arizona and the countless Celtic knots she embroiders. When I first met Caris, I asked her where she got the pendant, wondering if she was Irish like my mom. Caris just shrugged. "During one of my many travels," she'd said.

I shove my arms into the sleeves of her jean jacket. "Very chivalrous. How was Hawaii?"

She narrows her shiny eyes. "My mom spent more time getting slammed at the hotel bar than going to the beach. I'm still trying to erase the airplane ride from my memory."

For all her grace, Caris is ridiculously prone to motion sickness of any kind. She'd rather walk twenty miles than get into a car, much less fly across the Pacific to an island paradise.

"At least I made some new acquaintances," she says.

"Did you get their numbers?"

She runs a hand through her hair that's cropped to her chin. "Aren't you clever."

Caris makes friends wherever she goes. She's like a flame for moths, but she couldn't care less about keeping up with anyone. Other than me, that is. Guess that makes us twin flames, burning each other out and setting each other back on fire. Unlike me, though, she's got a great reputation. Or more like, no one thinks too much about her—bad or good. She blends in but sticks out. Kind of like her face. She's some ambiguous multiracial mixture that she never bothers to explain, and I'm not about to ask her parents where they came from.

"How's school?" she asks.

I shrug. "Brad's dtf."

"Again?" She tugs my arm, and we sit cross-legged on the dewy grass.

"He's definitely on my list of worst hookup choices ever."

She scoots till she's resting on her elbows, then changes her mind and throws her head into my lap. "Is there a list of best hookup choices?"

I think about her question for about half a second. "No."

"That's what I thought."

A few crickets are chirping in the distance, making music that sounds like someone hacking up a rhythmic cough. "I missed you at school."

"Of course you did," she says and shuts her eyes. "You see anything mystical in the hallways?"

"Not really."

She hums a weird tune that would never make it to the top of any hits list. "Let me stay the night," she says. "I don't feel like walking home."

"Get a car."

"Then I won't have any excuses," she says, but we both know we never need an excuse to see each other. Thunder loves lightning, and while Caris never cusses out teachers, or cuts holes in her designer jeans, she has to be electric to be my best friend.

❖

I found Caris under a tree near the school playground on a rainy morning. We were both in the third grade, and I had just gotten off the bus, walked into school, and left straight out the back door. At that time, I was still anxious about school buildings. I didn't like all the little gremlins hanging around in every corner or the trolls in the bathroom stalls. Everyone chalked it up to me being an only child with separation anxiety.

I sidled over to the playground, thinking that the yellow slide was a better way to pass the day than morning circle. I liked to play this game where I holed up inside the slide and screamed. If you haven't tried it, you won't understand. Your screams bounce off the walls, back into your ears but nobody else's.

The rain was pouring into my eyes, so I almost didn't see her. This small girl in a black raincoat, crouched low over a puddle. She was stirring leaves and branches into the mud. A silver necklace dangled from her neck and shimmered in the rain. A smudge of dirt marked her chin, and she had this air about her like she wanted to be alone.

So, of course, I decided to bother her. "What are you doing?" I asked. I even put my hands on my hips. After all, this weird girl was intruding on my playground.

When I spoke, she dropped her stick in the puddle. She had this surprised look on her face like she didn't know I could see her, but if she had wanted to hide, she'd picked a pretty bad spot.

"You're supposed to be in school," I told her.

Straightening her legs, she stood to about three-quarters my height. I guessed she might be in first or second grade. Still, her eyes met mine without any baby shyness. She sniffed, but I could tell she hadn't been crying. Her nose scrunched up as she wiped it with her raincoat sleeve, smearing mud across her face.

"So are you," she said in a small voice that somehow boomed louder than the thunder.

"Yeah, well, I'm going to the slide."

"Me too."

"No, you aren't."

"I am now." Believe it or not, she took *my* wrist and dragged me to the slide. We crawled inside, knees touching in the space that was barely big enough for the both of us. "What do we do now?" she asked.

"We scream." I showed her how, and Caris's dark eyes grew to saucers filled with delight. She didn't scream, but she laughed, and her laughter echoed into me until my eardrums hurt. Then the school bell sliced into our fun. We stumbled out onto the wet sand.

To my surprise, Caris followed me down the halls and to the door of my classroom. "Go away," I told her. "This class is for the big kids."

Instead of paying me any mind, she pushed open the door and stepped inside. I expected the teacher to be in a tizzy about my late arrival, and I'd even kidnapped one of the first graders, too, but Ms. Iman simply clapped her hands and put an affectionate arm around me.

"I was getting worried, Ashly," she cooed. "Thank you for finding our newest classmate. Everyone, please welcome Caris."

I think that was the only time my teacher told me thank you that whole year, but really, Caris was my gift to myself. You know you've found your soulmate when they listen to your screams and laugh.

❖

We're too old for slides now, so Caris and I take cover in the girls' restroom these days. We meet during fourth period on a pretty regular basis, because I take government with a boring teacher that teaches straight out of the textbook, and Caris has Spanish, which she claims to already know fluently. I'm waiting for her, seated on the automatic sink that likes to switch on every time I shift a bit to the left or right.

It's times like this that I wish I were one of those delinquent high schoolers that smoke cigarettes or vape in the bathroom. A few hits of nicotine could help me pass the minutes while I wait. I can't even text Caris to ask her when she can sneak off. To be honest, the only reason I don't vape is because of Caris.

The one time I took a pull of an e-cigarette, she yanked it out of my mouth and threw it straight in the trash. "You're literally inhaling iron into your lungs," she snapped, and since Caris never snaps, I figured I should listen to her. My parents could take a page from her book. All their *shoulds* pile up so high, I can't separate the good advice from the nagging.

The door creaks open, and Caris breezes in with her mouth pursed in annoyance. "When will teachers ever realize that no one is listening to them in the first place?" she says. Her jean jacket has slipped off her shoulder, revealing her bare arm.

"I'd rather read a textbook than listen to a lecture," I say.

I swing my legs back and forth, but she puts a hand on my knee, so I stop. She slides between my legs like she belongs there. She's the only one who I let this close to me when I'm sober.

"I wasn't aware that you read the textbooks."

I'd object, but she's right. "Homework is just knowing how to make good guesses."

"Clever as always."

Not half as clever as Caris, but I take the compliment. When I sit on the sink like this, she's at my eye level. Caris has this feel about her like she's taller than she actually is, but she's a head shorter than me. My thigh grazes her jeans, which are rough against my skin.

"Did you see any unexpected visitors before I arrived?" she says.

My eyes involuntarily dart to the corners of the bathroom, to the shadows cast by the stalls. "No, but I wasn't looking."

She nods. "So, what are we doing this weekend?" she asks, because Caris never has any plans unless her parents are dragging her somewhere. She doesn't keep up with any potential friends, remember? I'm holding the both of us up on the food chain.

The door creaks open again, and Jasmine Bennett saunters in. Just our luck. She sizes me and Caris up like someone eyeing an open trash bag on the curb. Without a word, she locks herself into a stall.

"Need some privacy, princess?" I say, because her stuck-up silent treatment grinds my gears.

"Sorry to break up your make-out session," she snaps back. The sound of her piss hitting the toilet water echoes off the tile walls.

Caris shakes her head, and I take her hint to back down. Jasmine is the kind of popular girl who watches too many teen movies and thinks that everyone in school worships her. Truth is, half the student body probably doesn't even know her name. What they do know is that she's the only girl at Hackley who can pull off red lipstick. She wears the same fire engine shade every day, like a siren wailing, *Look at me!*

As if on cue, she flushes and steps out of the stall with a lipstick tube in hand. She smears an extra layer on her lips. Her face is perfectly symmetrical, and I'm convinced that's the only reason she was nominated for homecoming court. Either that or the senior class was too scared of her to leave her name off the ballot.

"How are things going with Brad?" I ask in my most innocent voice. Given that Brad told the entire football team about our drunk hookup last spring break, she'll get my point. Our tête-a-tête took place during one of their infamous breakups.

With her lipstick reapplied, she takes a moment to admire her reflection. "Feel free to dine on my sloppy seconds," she says.

I'm a millisecond away from hopping off the sink, but Caris presses her palm into my thigh. A gentle reminder that another suspension might lead to a full-blown expulsion. Despite whatever the guidance counselors might believe, I do hope to graduate in June. Only a few months and a diploma away from liberation.

"Scamper along," I say through gritted teeth.

"I'll leave you two to whatever it is that I interrupted."

Her purse hits the door on her way out. She didn't even wash her hands. I'm left wondering how she and I grew up going to all the same schools, how we used to play doubles on the same tennis team. She and her parents play tennis at the same club where I meet with my instructor. Still, friendship isn't forged by proximity. Jasmine made it clear that we weren't meant to be long ago. But that's a story for another day.

"One day, I'll smear that lipstick all over her face," I say.

Caris tilts her head like a curious cocker spaniel. "Not worth your time, sweetheart."

Caris is also the only person I'd ever let get away with calling me sweetheart. Everyone probably thinks that we've been shacking since middle school, and no one would believe that we've never so much as kissed. I don't even know if Caris has ever kissed anyone, for that matter, guy or girl. One look at her, and anyone would think she could nab whoever she wanted. I've never chased anyone, and she's never broached the topic with me, so I figure that's a line we aren't crossing.

"Tell me what we're doing on Saturday," she says.

She'll go anywhere I ask her to go, but I'm never sure who's the one leading. She could've stayed playing in that puddle in the rain all by herself, and maybe that would have suited her just fine.

CHAPTER THREE

There's a secret lurking beneath my bad attitude. As it turns out, I'm out of my mind. Not in the fun way. Not in the throw-you-a-party way. And definitely not in the creative artist way. I see things other people don't see. You know how children make up imaginary friends? Or how nightmares can seem real when you open your eyes? Or how the long-departed haunt their loved ones? I don't see things like that, so don't even go there.

I've been *seeing* since I could rub two thoughts together and put names to faces and items and feelings. I'll be sitting at the dining room table, eating with Mom and Dad, but neither of them notices that we've got an extra guest with green skin and thorns for ears up on the countertop, swinging his legs while he listens to the seven o'clock news on the TV screen. I might be taking a trigonometry test, and while everyone else solves for the sum of the area of the circumference of six circles, I'm trying to ignore the girl with see-through wings and powder pink eyes that finds it funny to swap Mr. Spagnola's pencils with pens.

What's more: I'm almost positive that the things I'm seeing are real.

The only person who knows that I still see these things is Caris, and to be honest, I think she just puts up with it because she doesn't have any other friends. She wears this kind of knowing grin on her face when I point out a troll in the restroom or a sprite lighting up the night. Maybe it amuses her. Maybe she really believes me. What counts is that she never questions me about the faeries. She accepts this quirk of mine. That acceptance keeps me sane. Or at least partly sane.

Like today, for example, I'm changing clothes after tennis practice. Here in the Carson Tennis Club's locker room, there's a woman in the shower and another getting ready for a swim. Neither of them sees the shadow in the corner. Red eyes peek out from the edges of the black swarm. These kinds of faeries are the ones that unsettle me the most. The ones that lurk. The ones who are waiting to hurt.

I slip my skirt and shirt back on, stuff my tennis clothes in my duffel bag for a weekend wash, and hightail it out of the locker room. The shadow doesn't follow, but I'm sure another is close behind. That's the thing with seeing things. Once you notice them the first time, you keep seeing them. You start looking for them even when you don't want to.

I just want to go home, take a hot shower, and veg out in bed until Caris sneaks over, since I'm still grounded over grades. Confiscating my car keys was a smart move on my parents' part. It's limited the reach of sneaking out in the middle of the night. Then again, Caris doesn't like cars anyway.

I'm waiting for my Uber when my tennis instructor pulls her car up to the curb. Lanie has a zero-tolerance policy for giving her students a ride home, which means that she must have some parting words for me. Through the car window, I catch a glimpse of her slick ponytail and stern expression.

Sure enough, she rolls down the window. "Ashly, come here. Where are you headed?"

"Home," I say, more suspicious of her than ever.

"Straight home?"

Lanie and I have worked together since the seventh grade. She pushes me to ride a match out to the end, even when I feel like I'm losing. She brutally forces me into shuttle run tests when I'm operating on two hours of sleep, but she also sent me home early once to ice a sprained elbow that I tried to keep practicing on.

"Straight home," I say.

She nods slowly. "I've been trying to decide when and how to have this conversation with you. Your parents called me about your graduation status. Not just that, but your attendance is the worst it's been since freshman year. At some point, even club tournaments aren't going to tolerate this behavior."

I love Lanie, but I don't think the feeling is mutual these days. I can see it in her eyes when we rally. *You've hit a plateau,* she's saying. *Nothing is worse than coaching a plateau.* Between sporadic suspensions and spotty report cards, I can't play for a team. I don't qualify for most private tournaments. It's my fault, I know. Get it together, Ashly. Study more, Ashly. Make friends, Ashly. Find a good boyfriend, Ashly. Liking girls is a phase, Ashly. You just want attention, Ashly. What are you even doing with your time, Ashly?

An elf with blue skin and short jet-black hair steps beside me on the sidewalk. I groan, and Lanie raises an eyebrow, which means she thinks I'm groaning at her. The elf pokes me in the side, but I grit my teeth and try to listen to Lanie laying into me. The elf sneers, squinting his blood-colored eyes, and pulls a large, smooth stone from the leather bag on his hip.

"This is probably our last semester together," Lanie says. "At this point, you should be transitioning to a college team or adult tournaments. What's your plan, Ashly?"

The elf waves the stone in my face. I blink. If I ignore them, the faeries go away. Sometimes.

"I don't coach casual players," Lanie says.

The elf shrugs at my indifference, but he doesn't put the stone away. He steps directly in front of me, so I can't even see Lanie anymore. He lifts the stone. He aims for Lanie's windshield.

"Stop!" I shout. To my surprise, he shoves the stone back

in his pouch and prances off down the sidewalk. His laughter carries on the wind. It takes me a moment to figure out what he finds so funny. Lanie's mouth hangs open, fury written into her features. The elf's game of tricksy has succeeded.

"That kind of attitude is the exact reason why you'll never make it in tennis," Lanie says.

How am I supposed to respond to that? In Lanie's world, elves don't exist, much less throw rocks. The fae have been playing tricks and assigning me the blame since I could speak. But Lanie's words still sting me right in the eyes. I take a deep breath and push past it.

"So, I'll see you next week then?" I say.

"You're just wasting it all, Ashly. Stay out of trouble."

She drives off, and I decide that if I ever see that elf again, I'm gonna let him smash Lanie's windshield. Maybe.

❖

As the garbled dialogue of a late-night comedy show drifts down the hall, I pretend to be asleep in my bedroom. My bedside lamp casts its dark purple glow across two pairs of legs. Caris curls up on her side of the bed, eyes closed. I crack open my laptop and type *kinds of elves* into the search bar.

"He had blue skin," I say to Caris for the third time tonight. "I've never seen an elf like that."

Caris flips onto her back. "You see elves all the time. What does it matter if their skin is blue or white or gray?"

"He was gonna hurt Lanie."

Caris casts me an inquisitive look. I sigh, because I wasn't planning to tell her about my argument with Lanie. I already had to talk about it with my parents. I was two steps past the door when they told me she'd called them.

"It's been a while since you sighted a faerie trying to hurt someone," Caris says. I can never read between the lines with

Caris. She could be curious, or she could care. She might just want me to shut up and go to bed.

"Well, this guy had a rock aimed for her windshield. I made him stop, but you know how this sort of thing goes. Lanie thought I was telling her to stop lecturing me, and now I'm a bitch with an attitude problem."

"Are you a bitch?"

"C'mon, Caris."

Talking about Lanie has me grabbing a couple hard candies from my nightstand drawer. I reflexively offer some to Caris, but she's one of those health enthusiasts who avoids high fructose corn syrup and red dye at all costs. As I crack the candy between my teeth, I sift through the elf search results. A few minutes later, I find a fan page that catalogs faerie facts inspired by video games and kids' books and the darker, more obscure stuff. A drawing of a menacing yet beautiful face draws my attention. The caption reads: *Dark Elves*.

"Check this out," I tell Caris. To my surprise, she sits up beside me and peers at the paragraphs of faerie characteristics.

"Dark elves often have a blue-ish tint to their skin," she reads. "They love war and hate all other races of elves. Beautiful, terrifying, seductive, gifted in glamour and the art of possession. Also, never take food from them."

I roll my eyes. "That's obvious. We know that already. Faeries use glamour to hide themselves and trick humans, and I shouldn't take food from strangers, especially faeries."

Caris closes my laptop, which would be an invasion of my autonomy if it weren't her. "Tell me why we avoid food from faeries again."

"Humans who eat faerie food are asking to be turned into their puppets. At best, I'll get sick as a dog. At worst, I'll say or do anything they ask me to do. So don't go taking candy from strangers, Caris."

She smiles. "Your life is a fairy tale."

I don't know if she's amused or being condescending or feeling honest, but I let her take the laptop out of my hands and set it on the nightstand.

"Some fairy tale. I'm still waiting for a princess in shining armor to sweep me off my feet into the sunset."

Caris switches off the lamp. "She's coming."

"Thanks, Mom."

"Time for bed, sweetheart." Caris pulls me by the waist into the blankets. Her breath flutters against the bare skin of my shoulder, and I wonder why everything is so easy with Caris but a nightmare everywhere else.

"Let me take you somewhere tomorrow," Caris murmurs. Each word is a whisper on my skin. "Somewhere green. I know you hate dirt, but I promise it'll make up for the elf and your bad day with Lanie."

"Fine. Besides, it's a good excuse to say no to Brad's weekend invitation."

"Forget Brad." Caris's arm is warm around my torso. Her breathing gets heavy. In the living room, I hear the TV chime off and my parents' door click shut. It's quiet enough to hear my shallow breaths. To hear Lanie in my ears: *You'll never make it in tennis.* I'll never make it anywhere. I'm spending Friday nights on faerie websites and feeling sorry for myself when no one else can see.

Hot tears burn my eyes, and in the silence, I let them fall. As hard as I try, I can't stifle the sniffles, but Caris doesn't stir, so it's okay, I guess. I give myself a few minutes, and then I bite my tongue to stop the self-pity. Sure, I'm going nowhere in life, but crying isn't going to get me anywhere faster.

I wipe my snotty nose with the back of my hand. Even though all the tears are gone now, I'm still stuck with Lanie's voice in my head. Then Caris pulls me closer. I'm about to chalk it up to a dream till she says, "Time for sleep now."

Somehow, she can make anything happen.

CHAPTER FOUR

It's Saturday night, and I'm sitting, counting the minutes till Caris shows up. Since she doesn't have a phone, I have to trust her at her word that she's coming. Luckily, Caris has never lied to me. At least, I don't think she has ever lied to me. Or I've never found out.

A knock on my door has me throwing off my beanie and tucking my sneakers under my comforter. Mom steps in. Her brown hair is swept up in a messy bun. Tired eyes hide behind her frameless glasses.

"Hey, honey," she says like it's normal for her to check in at bedtime. "I'm about to head off to sleep."

"It's kind of late for you," I say. I grab a fitness magazine off my nightstand and flip through it in attempt at playing it cool.

Mom settles onto the bed, a little too close to my barely concealed sneakered feet for comfort. "I got a call from Aunt Erin about Grandma. She's back in the hospital again, but we're hoping it's only for a few days. She burnt herself while cooking."

"Is Grandma going to be okay?"

Aunt Erin and Grandma live in Phoenix, where my mom was raised. I saw them last summer when Grandma started chemotherapy. I remember sitting in the treatment center with her for two hours while Mom and Aunt Erin ran shopping errands. A clear bag of liquid medicine dripped down a tube and into her arm. Grandma kept her eyes closed most of the time, and I tried to ignore a small boy with goat legs who was sneaking sugar packets and cookies from a refreshments counter. At one point, Grandma looked up, and I swear she stared straight at the faerie when she said, "Too much of a sweet tooth is a bad thing."

"You want some cookies, Grandma?" I asked, but she only shut her eyes and smiled. For a moment, I felt like I wasn't crazy. But I wasn't brave enough to ask her if she saw the goat boy. What would have happened if she had said yes? Like anyone would ever say yes.

Mom sighs. "Grandma really shouldn't be cooking by herself anymore, but she's too stubborn to accept any at-home care. She took care of your grandpa till he passed away, and she thinks she can do the same for herself."

The fact that Mom is talking to me about this means that things must be pretty bad. "Maybe we could go visit again soon?" I say, mostly because I have no idea what else to say.

"I'm wondering that same thing." She pats my leg, then sizes up my gray sweats and orange hoodie. "Are you cold?"

Hoodies and sweats aren't my typical choice for pajamas. They're more like sneak out in the middle of the night attire. I say a silent prayer that Caris doesn't knock on my window right now.

"I haven't been feeling too great today," I lie, which makes me feel bad, especially since Mom isn't having the best night. "I've had this tension headache that's giving me the chills."

She places a hot hand on my forehead. "You don't feel warm," she says.

"It's nothing. I'll be better in the morning."

Mom nods and stands back up. "Well, make sure to go to bed soon and get some rest."

"Same to you."

She cracks a smile at my concern, then heads out the door.

I breathe a sigh of relief and toss the fitness magazine back on my nightstand. My thoughts are caught somewhere in between my good luck and Grandma's poor health when my window starts to open on its own. Caris's shadow fills the frame.

"You scared me," I hiss as she climbs into the room.

"What? You expecting someone else?"

My bedside lamp casts its purple glow across her playful grin. I can't help but smile back, even if her comment was a little dry. My lack of witty response fills the room with silence. I expect Caris to deliver another sarcastic remark, but she slides onto the bed instead. Her hand grazes the blanket that still covers my sweats and sneakers.

"Are you ready for an adventure tonight?" she says.

"Depends. Just how much dirt is involved in this expedition? All my sneakers are white."

Caris never rolls her eyes. Instead, she closes them, like she can't be bothered to endure others' senselessness for a moment longer. I have never seen anyone else make such a condescending, yet alluring, expression. So, naturally, it pisses me off when she crosses her arms and shuts her eyes in response to my aversion to dirt. It also annoys me that my heart inexplicably skips a beat once her eyes reopen and her gaze lands directly on mine.

"I think you can handle a picnic in the woods."

"How romantic," I say sarcastically.

Caris hops off the bed. "Off we go, little Ashly. You can back out later if your dirt-to-prissy ratio gets too high to handle."

I'm about to throw off my blanket and give her the middle finger at the same time when there's another knock on the door. Caris glances to the open window, but there's no time. The doorknob is turning. I shut off my bedside lamp, and Caris backs into the corner between the wall and my nightstand. The streetlamps are just bright enough to outline her figure.

We are so busted.

Mom comes in with a glass and what looks like a bottle of medicine in hand. In the dark, I can barely make out her face, but it looks like her glasses are off. It's the tiniest thread of hope that I'll make it out of this disaster without another month added to my lifetime sentence of being grounded.

"Were you headed to sleep?" she asks. "You switched off the light."

"Gotta give in to the sandman eventually." I lace my voice with mock-sleepiness and pull my blanket closer to my chin.

"Well, I brought you some ibuprofen for your headache and a little water. You never drink enough water."

Mom is being such a kind soul tonight that it makes me wish I wasn't trying to sneak out. Just as the guilt starts to gut me, she rounds the bed, passes the open window, and heads for my nightstand. Right next to Caris. There's no way to stop her short of jumping out of bed and directly between the two of them. That seems like a worse way to go than simply letting this fiasco unfold.

Except, Mom doesn't even glance at the open window. She places the glass of water on my nightstand and twists open the medicine bottle. While she may not be wearing her glasses, I cannot believe that she doesn't notice Caris standing right behind her.

"Are you all right, honey?" she says.

I realize I'm gawking in Caris's direction. So, I straighten up my face and take the medicine from Mom's outstretched hand. "Thanks for the ibuprofen. This headache is the worst."

I swear Caris laughs under her breath. If I could, I'd throw my pillow straight at her nose. Instead, I'm downing a couple of pills for the sake of the charade. Mom has to be one hundred percent worried about Grandma, because she's still somehow unaware of Caris's presence.

"Love you," she says.

"Love you, too."

When Mom finally leaves, I do throw the pillow at Caris,

but of course she catches it midair and throws it right back at my face. "Hey!" I say.

She puts a finger to her mouth with a grin as wide as the Cheshire Cat. "Don't shout. You want her to come back and check on you again?"

I bite back the urge to point out her incriminating laugh from earlier. Caris grabs my wrist and pulls me from the bed. I stuff an extra pillow under the blanket in case Mom really does come back. Then we slip out the window, into the chilly night, and on our way to whatever muddy madness Caris thinks is a good way to spend a Saturday night.

❖

After a half mile of walking, a thousand turns through neighborhood streets, and an unmarked stretch of gravel road, Caris stops us in front of a chain link fence.

"We jump this, and we're almost there."

Before I can complain, she's halfway up the fence. I'm not about to be left behind, so I follow. When we land on the other side, our feet thud into the soft earth. Our breath comes out in white puffs. I'm glad I grabbed my orange beanie before we left. The cold, humid air seems to have the opposite effect on Caris. Her eyes shine in the starlight, which I didn't even know was possible.

"One more thing," she says, more to herself than to me. She takes a few steps along the fence, then picks up something indistinguishable in the dark. I turn on my phone flashlight, which uncovers a wicker picnic basket.

"You really went out of your way."

Caris shrugs. "I promised you a good time."

With that, she ushers us away from the fence and into a wooded area. While it looks foreboding at this time of night, the woods are most likely connected to our town's five-acre recreational park. I've endured a science project or two out this deep in Kit Park, but that was in the middle of the school day. Caris could very well lead us into the jaws of a mountain lion right now, but she's doing it with such confidence that it seems more foolish to turn around than to follow.

That is, until I hear the squelch of slick earth beneath my white sneakers.

"Caris—"

"How about here?" she says.

A grassy hill rises from a circle of groaning trees. The sky is clear above the hill, and the whole scene is straight out of a picture book. Still, I'm not about to let Caris get her way so easily. I fake a heavy sigh, but she ignores me and heads straight for the top of the hill.

I turn my flashlight back on. Sure enough, mud is caked past the soles of my sneakers and into the laces. Yet as Caris spreads a Hackley High School blanket over the damp grass, I realize I no longer care. Squeaky-clean tennis shoes and primly ironed tennis skirts, top-notch athlete grades and perfect dynamics with a coach—out here in the middle of nowhere, all of that somehow fades away. I take the deepest breath I've taken in weeks.

Caris motions me toward her. I kick off my shoes and sit cross-legged on the blanket. When she reaches back into the basket, I hope she unearths a bottle of wine. Instead, she sets out plastic containers filled with fruit and honey and a clear water bottle full of a mystery blue liquid.

"Almost classy," I say. "I'm guessing that's liquor with some kind of chaser made from *raw* sugar?"

Caris takes a sip from the water bottle, then passes it to me. A burst of berry sweetness explodes on my tongue. It tastes nothing like alcohol, yet my chest is already warm.

"It's from back home," she says.

"I didn't realize your parents were big juicers." I've met Tim and Tina dozens of times at back-to-school nights and while hanging out at Caris's house. Beyond a slight physical resemblance, Caris seems about as far as the apple can fall from the tree.

Caris stares past me and into the woods, like her parents might step out any moment. She takes another drink from the water bottle. "I didn't say they made it."

The silence that settles between us overflows with the calls and shuffling of nocturnal wild things. Instead of getting scared, I sip at the juice-that-isn't-juice. The warmth buzzes into my brain. Caris dips a strawberry into honey, tips back her head, and takes a bite that is more than a little over-the-top. I'm about to tease her for it when the lights blink on.

We're in the middle of the forest, so there aren't any streetlamps or electrical lines. Still, small globes of light start flickering between the trees. At first, there's only four or five. Then, slowly but surely, the lights multiply, until we're surrounded by twinkling, incandescent ornaments.

"Wow," I whisper, trying to take it all in.

"Wow?"

Caris raises an eyebrow. She can't see the glowing lights, even though they're bright enough to illuminate the blue liquid in the bottle she's holding. Her dark hair and eyes gleam as the spheres languidly float around us. I catch a glimpse of a tiny faerie inside one of the lights. Her iridescent wings shiver as she passes by.

"They're everywhere," I say.

"The faeries?" Caris looks to the left and right, then back to me. "Tell me what you see."

I stare at her hard, because this is another of those many moments when I wonder whether Caris believes in my Sight. Her lips are turned up just a little. Her eyes stay on mine, and I choose to lean in, if only to feel a little less alone.

"There are small faeries—pixies, I think. They're glowing, like café lights, but way more beautiful. The forest is full of

them. There's one right behind you." Caris turns and the pixie
darts away mischievously. "One just flew into the basket. And
another one is trying to take a strawberry."

I laugh and shoo the faerie away with my hand. Caris
laughs, too. I'm not sure what she finds funny, because she
can't see what I see. Then she says, "It's breathtaking, isn't
it?"

My heart squeezes. "I wish you could really see it."

Caris tilts toward me. Her hand brushes the tips of my
hair. Her fingertips trace the crook of my neck. "There's one
on your shoulder."

When I check, there's nothing but empty air.

"It flew away." She passes me the bottle, then leans back
on her elbows. "This is the perfect way to spend a Saturday
night."

I take a sip, feeling the juice's heady warmth. It's a little
nice to have a friend who is willing to play along. Nice, but also
a little sad. I close my eyes on the pixies and Caris, knowing
full well that I'll be cold and alone once again by the morning.

CHAPTER FIVE

I'm sitting in homeroom, minding my own business on a boring Monday morning, when Mr. Diaz decides to violently attack us all with graduation status reports. Well, he passes them out pretty gently, placing them upside-down on our desks. The intercom switches on, and Jasmine Bennett's voice drifts into the room.

"Good morning, Hackley High School," she says, but it's not a good morning. With it being her turn as the student council member to read the announcements, I can't help but think it's a bad omen for another rotten school day.

I don't have to turn over the status report to know what it says: *You're screwed.* Except it doesn't say that. It eloquently explains that I have almost enough credits, but I'm currently failing two subjects. There's also a warning that my attendance is shot, so I'd better not miss any more classes. Otherwise, I might never earn a diploma, or earn a future, for that matter.

When the announcements come to a close, I'm still staring at the status report. Everyone else has put theirs down, and they're horsing their way through the last half of homeroom. My parents have to sign this. No doubt they're going to tell Lanie. I don't want to sit through another post-practice lecture or living room reprimand.

I don't want to go home.

But I don't want to be in this classroom either. Even though there's only ten minutes before the bell, I ask Mr. Diaz for the bathroom pass. He shrugs and tells me to just take my bookbag and go. He doesn't have to tell me twice.

I'm halfway to the water fountain when Jasmine Bennett appears around the corner. She must be on her way back to homeroom after reading the announcements in the main office. I'm not in the mood, so I plan to just ignore her. Thankfully, her nose is stuck in her cell phone. But the moment she passes me, her hostility radar must go off. She slips her phone in her back pocket. Her eyes glint like an owl swooping in for a rabbit, which is ridiculous because we both know my talons are sharper than hers.

"Ditching?" she asks. "Where's your pass?"

"Student council and hallway patrol? You keep yourself busy these days."

I head down the hallway, hoping she'll go to the bathroom or something and we can just call it a day, but she follows me. "I was looking at the club schedule for the courts," she says. "Looks like we're both practicing on Fridays after school now. Maybe our instructors will let us play a few rounds."

I frown. Jasmine plays varsity tennis. I haven't played on the same team as her since I lost the privilege to be in JV back in the ninth grade. Apparently, ditching class and cussing a few too many times in front of the school principal are supposed to be indicators of poor athletic performance. Being on Jasmine's team stopped appealing to me before I was kicked off, though. Our rivalry-meets-friendship collapsed halfway through junior high. Unfortunately, she still takes extra lessons from a private instructor at Carson Tennis Club, so sometimes we run into each other in the locker room whenever the universe is feeling especially venomous toward me.

I keep walking, but Jasmine is hot on my heels. "Maybe if you focused less on stalking my tennis schedule," I say over my shoulder, "you might actually make some progress in your overhead shots."

"Says the one who can't even sit in a desk for long enough to earn a spot on any team," she lashes back. The fact that she's so riled up means I guessed right. Her overhead shots must still be weak.

Before I can bask in the satisfaction of hitting her where it hurts, she adds, "I still can't believe they didn't ban you from Carson for what you did back in middle school."

I whip around, and Jasmine falls back a few steps. "You mean for what *you* did to me back in middle school."

"I saw it with my own eyes. You opened all the lockers and threw everyone's clothes in the showers. I didn't do anything."

"You lied."

She laughs. "Don't tell me you still believe that some magical creatures did it?"

"You saw it."

Jasmine scrunches her eyebrows and purses her lips in an awful smile meant for cooing over puppies that still can't open their eyes. "You're still obviously out of your mind. You go around acting like you're better than everyone else, but the truth is you're a freak that sees things that aren't real."

I'm about to shove her into the nearest locker, but she flits past me too quickly. Before turning down another hall, she says, "Don't forget to carry a pass next time," like the whole conversation never happened. Like I'm the one causing trouble in the halls. I just wanted some fresh air and a drink of water.

I'm taking deep breaths and wishing for the zillionth time in my life that I could text Caris, when I hear footsteps headed for me from around the corner that Jasmine just turned. Part of me prepares for her to come back and finish the fight, but the footsteps aren't right. They've got a strange skip to them that no student or teacher would have.

Instinctively, I start backing up. My eyes are glued to the corner. An unnaturally dark shadow starts pooling on the sidewalk. Then leather boots emerge, fastened to uncannily long legs. Black, feathered trousers fall from a leather vest with a tall feather collar. Long, raven hair spills down milk-blue shoulders. Cold eyes, the lifeless color of a wintry ocean, bore into mine.

Except for the eyes and clothes, this faerie looks nearly identical to the one that attacked Lanie, but with none of his impishness. She's staring daggers at me like I killed her firstborn, and every nerve in my body screams: *Run*. I dash past a long row of lockers. The faerie's strange skip follows me down the hall. My sneakers squeal as I halt in front of a closed classroom, and I barely register the number on the door before I push my way through.

Of course, it's Mrs. Carmel's homeroom. That means it's Caris's homeroom, which almost sounds like an awesome coincidence, and it would be, if not for an awful accompaniment: Bradley Jameson shares a homeroom with Caris.

"Can I help you, Ms. Harris?" Mrs. Carmel asks me with enough tone to tell me she wants me out faster than I came barreling in. I glance to Caris. She's casually leaned back in her desk chair, all loose like she's used to me strolling into her homeroom. But her eyes are narrow, and my stomach flips, because that's the rare face that Caris makes only when she's concerned.

"Ashly just couldn't wait to me see me, I guess," Brad calls out from his desk in the back.

Brad and Jasmine are clearly meant for each other. "Fuck off, Brad," I say. Then I remember my graduation status and regret it.

Mrs. Carmel stares me down with enough malice to almost make me forget the dark elf in the hallway. Thankfully, the faerie hasn't chased me into the room. One less problem to deal with for now.

Mrs. Carmel crosses her arms. "It's a Monday, Ms. Harris, and it's only 8:20 a.m. Let me at least finish my coffee before I write my first detention for the week."

While Brad obviously started the detention-worthy trouble, I'm not in the position to point that out. Luckily, it's 8:20 a.m., just like Mrs. Carmel said, so the bell rings. Everyone grabs their things. Mrs. Carmel grabs her coffee tumbler and shoos all of us, including me, out with her free hand.

There are no faeries in the hall. Just the sound of lockers banging and laughter falling from open mouths. Brad dares to wink at me before hightailing into the crowd. We don't have any classes together this semester, so hopefully I can avoid him for the rest of the week. Or else I might wind up suspended by then.

Caris sidles up to me. She kicks my foot with hers, which snaps me out of whatever funk I'd stumbled into. I let out a sigh. At least half the weight of this morning tumbles off my shoulders. Caris does that to me. We start walking toward the portable classrooms on the other side of the school.

"You just couldn't wait to see me, I guess," Caris says, quoting Brad from earlier.

"As much as I absolutely adore you, my dear, I had other reasons to crash your homeroom. There was another dark elf."

Caris stops mid-step. We're halfway through the quad, and I remember that her locker is on the other side of campus. She doesn't have her backpack or any books in hand, and Mr. Campbell always expects us to bring our English notebooks to class. Still, she grabs my wrist and leads me to the portable classrooms. Instead of ushering us toward English, she pulls me to a secluded spot where the backside of two classrooms meet. A chunky layer of paint coats the wall behind us, covering first semester's graffiti. Barely a month into the New Year, someone's already scrawled *YOLO* in black Sharpie. Another smaller message reads, *Smile: You're on camera.*

"Tell me what happened." Caris's eyes are narrow again.

"Jasmine was talking trash in the hall. Then she ran off, but a dark elf appeared out of nowhere." I try to keep my voice casual and convincingly even. "It's nothing, right?"

Caris frowns. That's it. She leans against the wall, frowns, and fiddles with her silver necklace. I'm stuck wondering if she's thinking I need to go back to therapy. Not that therapy wouldn't help me handle all this stuff with graduation and tennis and my failure of a future, but my old therapist back in middle school fixated more on the faeries and less on my actual life problems. A small part of me questions whether I might be cracking under the stress. I can almost hear what my therapist might say, *These dark faeries seem to come out whenever you're in the middle of a conflict. First, Lanie. Now, Jasmine.* That nagging thought—the one I've spent years stuffing down—rises to the surface with a vengeance: *What if I'm really hallucinating?*

Caris reaches for me again, her palm warm against my forearm. "Don't do anything rash with that elf," she says, like I might mouth off to faeries in the middle of the hallway. She has to think I'm completely delusional.

I try to laugh it all off. "You could have just lied and told me everything is peachy keen."

"Could I?" Caris's hand trails back down to my wrist. Then she shakes her head and releases my arm. When her gaze settles on mine, my heart trips again. We're alone, but she and I are alone together all the time. So, why is my pulse flying ten miles a minute?

The warning bell rings, which means we've only got one minute till first period. Even though we're in the same class, Caris no doubt needs to go to her locker. I want to tell her to stay. I want to trade jokes until I forget about the dark elf completely, but she's already several steps away, headed toward the quad.

I can't keep her with me. We're at school, and class rules and the school bell always have the last laugh. My graduation status report is evidence of that. Caris waves over her shoulder, like I never mentioned the faeries in the first place. I turn toward class. I don't know how I'm supposed to walk into English and raise my GPA with all the shadows on my mind.

CHAPTER SIX

I arrive to tennis practice early, so early in fact that Lanie hasn't made it to the court yet. I bounce the tennis ball on the asphalt as I wait. I crack my neck. There's no wind and little humidity. The temperature is perfect, and the sun peeks through just the right amount of cloud coverage.

I'm so tired. Since Mom and Dad sat me down on the porch swing a week and a half ago and delivered a heart-to-heart about my graduation status, I've been walking around shackled to the weight of *life after graduation.* Jasmine will probably be recruited by a Division I tennis team at a top-notch university. Caris always manages to joke her way around her college plans, but I'm just biding my time till she shows up with an acceptance letter. I even overheard Brad saying he's choosing between USC and Stanford.

My resolution is to go to all my classes for the rest of the third quarter. I'm not sure whether that will make a difference, though. After all, when I raised my hand to answer an easy question in trig this morning, Mr. Spagnola called on me by saying, "Someone's already gone to the restroom. Wait till they come back."

At least I came to practice early. Even though I'm exhausted, I can always summon up energy for practice. This court is the only place where I can truly come alive. When my racket hits a ball, when I'm focused in on my opponent's next move, I can finally toss aside all my failures. I can breathe.

Lanie opens the gate and steps onto the court. She's got a visor on, but that can't shield her surprise that I beat her to practice.

"Haven't seen you this early since ninth grade," she says, but the smile on her face speaks miles more. I don't think I've seen her smile at me like that since ninth grade either, not since I was kicked off Hackley's JV team.

After a quick warm-up, Lanie launches us into a baseline rally. She starts off with an overhead serve. With short steps, I fine-tune my position and return with a forehand stroke. Like clockwork, the ball zooms down the middle of the court, but there's no use patting myself on the back for one return.

Lanie's forehand swing is stronger than mine. Still, she's keeping things cool with groundstrokes. The ball bounces toward me. Practice has only just started, and I'm feeling great already. We continue our rally until a minor misstep on Lanie's end winds up gifting me the first point.

"Twenty-second recovery," she says.

My breath crashes like an ocean in my chest as I pace the back of the court. I count the seconds against my racing heart. My whole body feels light, but a memory of the JV team flashes in my mind. The disappointment that shrouded my parents as I told them the bad news. The tears I swallowed and turned into screams when they sent me to my room. But Caris was waiting for me on the bed. I stumbled into her arms, and she rubbed circles into my shoulders. I bit my tongue to hold back the tears, but dry sobs still wracked my chest.

"Ashly," Caris whispered into my hair. "Want me to sneak into the principal's office and forge you a new school record?"

She could always make me laugh through the worst moments. "How about you make me a better person while you're at it."

"That's easy." Caris snapped in front of my nose. "Hmm, nothing changed. I guess you were already the best."

Twenty seconds fly by. "Your serve," Lanie says.

I'm fine with just me and Lanie. Playing singles in private leagues has been better than nothing. I'm far from being nothing.

I curve my fingertips around the lime-green fuzz of the ball. After I toss it into the air, I relish the sound of the wind through my racket as I shoot the ball over the net. I glance to Lanie, preparing myself for her return.

My breath snags in my throat. Lanie isn't alone on her side of the court. One of the dark elves stands directly behind her. His red eyes meet mine with the same ferocity as the faerie I fled from at school. A wolfish grin reveals his pointed teeth.

The ball hits my side of the court, but I miss it completely, my eyes glued to the dark elf.

Lanie clucks her tongue just loud enough for me to hear. "Stay on your toes," she says. All I can manage is a nod in response because the faerie is coming closer to Lanie. He reaches out slender, blue fingers toward her shoulders. A shiver knifes through my spine.

"Back off!" I shout.

The elf sneers as Lanie crosses her arms. "Not this again, Ashly," she says.

"No, it's not like that…I'm sorry."

Lanie shakes her head, then grabs a spare ball and starts up the rally again. I try to focus on her serve, on my positioning, on the placement of my racket, but the faerie is stalking down the side of the court. His red eyes watch me intently.

With my attention split, I stand no chance against Lanie. I lose the point again, and I can't even meet Lanie's disappointed gaze. I've got twenty seconds to come up with some kind of plan to get rid of the elf. I pace to the corner of the court. When I turn around, he's waiting for me. We meet in the center of the court.

"I said back off," I whisper, so Lanie won't hear.

"Never, mortal," he hisses. For years, the faeries have laughed at me, they've caused mischief, and even swept my notebooks off my school desk. This is the first time that I have feared for my life.

He seizes my racket, winding his fingers in the strings. On impulse, I tighten my grip and yank, but for all his leanness, I'm clearly outmatched. I pull as hard as I can, and he tugs back with that wolfish, condescending sneer.

Then, as suddenly as he grabbed my racket, he lets go. I fall backward, landing painfully on the ground. Maybe it's the adrenaline, maybe it's my attitude problem, or maybe I have a death wish, but I jump back up and throw my racket straight for his face.

I don't think I've ever won against a faerie, and this elf is no different. He side-steps the racket faster than a jumping spider, then bares his sharp teeth once again.

"You're throwing full-blown tantrums now?" Lanie shouts. Her hands are on her hips, and she's headed straight for me. For us. Somehow, I'm going to have to protect Lanie from this dark elf that she can't even see.

But when I turn back to the wolfish elf, he's gone. Not like *poof!* gone. The tennis court gate clangs shut, which means he just walked away. So now I'm left here with Lanie glaring at me. My tennis racket is still on the asphalt, where I threw it, and no one would ever believe that a faerie was here just moments before.

"You need to cool it," Lanie says. "Go get some water and come back when you've calmed down."

I'm only fifteen minutes into practice, and let's be real, it's already over. I guzzle my water so fast that I choke, or it could be rage that closes my throat. As coughs wrack through me, I can't help but wonder what would have happened if I'd let the elf mess with Lanie. Instead of taking the blame, I could let the chaos unfold. It might even feel good.

❖

I'm staring down the long corridor lined with doors to equipment closets, a humming generator, and eventually the locker rooms. The walls echo with the distant rip of zippers and the far-off spray of showers. My white polo is cold with sweat. The air conditioner freezes my legs in place.

This corridor should feel like a second home, but today it's full of nightmares. Or, not quite nightmares, because bad dreams aren't real, and my memories of Carson Tennis Club are one hundred percent factual. Some people just remember the facts differently than I do.

I was thirteen years old. Tennis was the glove that perfectly fit my hand. I'd learned to hold a racket before learning how to read. Tennis was fun and easy, and I was *good* at it. There was even a faerie or two that would toss me balls in my backyard. Of course, when I told my parents about the faeries, they laughed off my vivid imagination. If I pointed out the pixies lighting up a tennis court at sunset, my coaches scolded me to be more serious. My fourth-grade teammates giggled at my detailed descriptions of dwarfs inside the changing room lockers. They threw their T-shirts over their flat-chested sports bras and cried, "Don't make jokes about peeping toms!"

Every once in a while, Mom or Dad would cast a wary eye my way when I stared at an empty tree for too long or when I shouted angrily at a vacant space in the bleachers. I earned a *Needs Improvement* mark on my fifth-grade citizenship report card for talking during tests, but I always insisted that I couldn't help it. Faeries were and are everywhere, but for my eyes only. The faeries always seem to know this, and they find it endlessly entertaining.

What's fun for a faerie is bad news for the rest of us. I was thirteen years old, and Jasmine Bennett and I were playing doubles together. Our instructors lavished us with enough attention to stir up both a deep love for being paired together and a secret jealousy for one another's skills. Jasmine's agility and endurance complemented my technique and proficiency. We often stayed later than the others at practice, pressuring each other into endless rallies, refusing to be the first to quit.

It was after one of these long Saturday practices that Jasmine found her true edge over me. We carelessly dropped our rackets onto the locker room floor, changing T-shirts over rumbling stomachs. Dinner would be on the table by the time Dad picked me up and parked us in the driveway. I was daydreaming about Salisbury steak when the showers switched on.

Jasmine and I were the only ones in the locker room. Naturally, we were pretty freaked out.

"Who's there?" I asked. I tiptoed closer to the showers, while Jasmine cowered behind.

"Stop messing with me," Jasmine said to me. "You're just upset that I played better than you today."

Snatches of laughter bounced off the tile walls. "Did you hear that?" I asked Jasmine, but she only shook her head.

A sprite spun out of the shower. Water flew off her iridescent wings. She stood shorter than me, but her features were those of a grown woman. Leaves covered her body, woven together into a dress that stopped short of her knees. This wasn't the first sprite I'd seen. They were generally harmless, but also nonsensical, restless, and prone to mischief.

The sprite took one long look at me and Jasmine and found us unworthy of her playtime. Then our eyes met. In an instant, she realized I could see her, and suddenly, Jasmine and I became her perfect audience. Faeries are like that. They spend all their time hiding from humans and pulling tricks in corners. Yet, the moment they're busted, their insidious nature quickly breaks the surface.

As the sprite made a dive for the lockers, a gasp escaped my mouth, but I bit back any words. I thought for sure the sprite would burn herself on the locker's metal handle. By this time, I'd discovered that faeries hated the touch of iron on their bare skin. They might kick open my backyard gate with their boots, but bare fingertips to a doorknob made them screech. They snuck through doors left partway open to bring in the groceries, or through windows letting in the breeze.

I shouldn't have worried. The sprite whipped out a branch from beneath her dress and began prying open the locker with its pointed end. She tittered as the handle popped up.

"What's happening?" Jasmine asked. She couldn't see or hear the faerie, but the faerie must not have glamoured the locker creaking open.

I was old enough to know that no one believed in faeries. I didn't know what to tell Jasmine, but the absolute terror that paled her face churned up chunks of guilt in my gut.

The sprite continued her rampage, skipping over the few lockers with combination locks. Soon, every locker without a lock yawned open, revealing several bags and shoes and changes of clothes and extra equipment. Her fists grasped a pair of sneakers and a hoodie.

"Is it a ghost?" Jasmine clutched my arm and ducked behind me. From her perspective, clothes and tennis balls floated through the air on their own. The hodgepodge drifted to the shower drain, muddled together in a wet mess.

A symphony of sports gear sailed from the lockers to the showers. Even Jasmine's clothes and bag joined the tangle. The sprite approached my locker and untucked my brand-new tennis jacket. I'd been begging for that jacket for months.

I charged at the faerie. She cackled and flung my jacket into the air before running out the door. Clutching the jacket to my chest like a prize, I shut my eyes and leaned against the lockers. Footsteps filled the room, as I thought, *I'm not giving this jacket up, no way.* But the sprite never returned. Jasmine's mom entered the locker room. She'd probably wondered what was taking her daughter so long. Whatever chiding she'd prepared for Jasmine dissipated like smoke off a snuffed flame as she took in the open lockers, the running shower, and the wayward tennis balls that had escaped the sprite's shenanigans.

"What happened here?" Mrs. Bennett gasped.

I glanced at Jasmine, who watched me closely. Something dangerous flickered in the set of Jasmine's eyes, in the sly tilt of her head. This expression of hers usually showed up whenever the coach scolded me or I lost a point in a single.

"Ashly did it," Jasmine said.

Mrs. Bennett loomed over me disapprovingly, arms crossed.

"No!" I said. "It was the faerie!"

Looking back, I should've lied and blamed Jasmine, and then we both would have taken the fall. After all, a mean little lie is often easier to digest than the truth. When the hallway camera footage showed only a few elderly women leaving the locker room before Jasmine and I went in, my fate was sealed. Jasmine became our team's only star player. I was disqualified for the rest of the season, and my story about the faerie put me in therapy three times a week.

I insisted that faeries were real for about a month, but that led to talks of medicine and hospitalization. Mom was beside herself, begging me to stop blaming faeries and just admit my wrongdoings. My parents didn't want to accept that their only child might need a lifetime of therapy for hallucinations, and they would never believe that I could really see faeries. Buried beneath my therapist's interrogations and my parents' demands, I started questioning whether or not I had actually been the one to trash the locker room. No one could see faeries but me. What were the odds that I was that special? But if I stopped believing in the faeries, then I'd have to accept the only other alternative.

Eventually, they promised me a private tennis instructor if only I would admit to my misdeeds. I picked putting an end to their questions. I picked being left alone. I picked a tennis instructor over faeries. Tennis never landed me in therapy. Even when I shouted and screamed for my parents and therapist to believe me, they only stared back with sad eyes. They didn't want an angry little girl who could see faeries. They wanted things to be easy. They wanted a lie. And lying is what made everyone happy.

Faeries made me into a freak.

Even now, walking down this empty corridor and into the locker room, I know: It doesn't matter if faeries are real or not. What matters is living up to others' expectations. Jasmine made me the villain, so I'll keep up the gimmick. It's easier than being honest. It's easier than getting hurt.

CHAPTER SEVEN

The sun is halfway under the horizon by the time I exit my Uber. Caris is leaning against the wood post of my mailbox. Her hands hide in her jean jacket pockets, and the smirk on her lips forewarns some kind of escapade. I might not be in the mood. Then again, the weight on my heart lifts a bit when our eyes meet. Going home, sitting alone in my bedroom with nothing but bad memories for company would be a worm in the rotten apple of this day. Or I could follow Caris down a fresh path. Even if that path leads to more trouble.

"Why didn't you just meet me at the tennis club?" I say.

"Not my territory." In all these years, Caris has never taken up a sport. She's fit but completely disinterested. According to Caris, team sports are pointless, and she'd rather go mucking about the woods or whatever it is she does in her free time. That is, when she's not with me.

I drop my tennis bag in the driveway. "Whatever trouble you're wanting to stir up tonight, I'm not game. I'm still grounded, and practice was a nightmare today."

"Everyone who can't fly is grounded," she says. "What happened at practice?"

I sigh. "A dark elf showed up. The one that looks like a boy, but he acts like he's a wolf on the prowl. His clothes were even made from this material that looks like black fur, but the girl elf I saw at school wears feathers."

"So, we'll call him Wolf, and we'll call her Raven."

"We're giving them names now? What are they, my pet faeries?" I lean against the mailbox beside Caris, and she laughs so suddenly that I laugh, too. Caris always knows how to make me laugh. It may be the first time I've laughed today.

"They're more like wild animals," I add. "Wolf straight up attacked me today, and Lanie thought I had a meltdown from her critiques."

I'm about to go into detail when I catch the shock coming off Caris in waves. Apparently, a full-blown fight with a faerie is too much for even Caris to handle.

"I get it," I say. "I probably should've just ignored the elf and played tennis, but he freaks me out and—"

The words die in my throat. As if Wolf wasn't enough for one day, a troupe of gnomes comes dawdling down the empty street. Matching blue tunics, pointed red caps, long white beards, the whole shebang. They march in a straight line, and I swear their leader is muttering *hup, hup!* under his breath.

Caris follows my glare as the gnomes tramp up my driveway.

"Hey! I can see you, you know. Get off my property!"

The gnomes trade agitated whispers. Then their leader snickers, and the whole bunch books it for my front porch. The gnomes hoist one another up onto the porch swing. It's pretty harmless, but they've caught me on a bad day.

Caris looks toward the porch and clicks her tongue. "Some little guys are causing mischief, huh?"

"Tell me you see that, right? You can see the porch swing moving?"

"The wind is in their sails."

"For real, Caris, do you see it?"

She links her arm in mine. "Let's go make our own mischief. I heard there's a revel tonight, and we should make an appearance. I'm bored, and if I go home too early, Tim and Tina will beg me to watch old-time TV with them again."

My parents aren't home yet, but by the time Dad leaves the office and Mom drives home from grocery shopping after work, Lanie will have contacted them in whatever group message they maintain for my sake. That means more scolding. At this point, my grounding sentence is nearing fifty years to life, and I'm one more lecture away from starting a home-imprisonment strike. Besides, I'm wrongly accused, as always. Wolf belongs under house arrest, not me. I feel a flush of anger at the injustice.

"By revel you mean the regular crowd at the Kit Park Playground?" I say, happy to be distracted.

"Our options are limited."

With Caris's arm still twined around mine, I pick my tennis bag off the ground. "Let me change clothes. How much you want to bet both Jasmine *and* Brad will be there."

"If we run into both of them, then I promise to walk you home."

"You'd walk me home anyway. I want a real bet."

"Isn't it nice knowing I'll walk you home for sure, though?"

As we head up the driveway, the gnomes wave at me from the porch swing. "Wait, does that mean you won't walk me home if they aren't there?"

"You better hope Jasmine and Brad show up."

Despite her carefree façade, Caris loves drama. So, she's gotta love me, right?

❖

The architect behind Kit Park Playground clearly had a passion for the bizarre, all in the hopes of building an award-winning playground for kids. A jungle gym, tube slides, tire swings, monkey bars, and a merry-go-round jut from the ground in the typical fashion. The artistry shows up in the gargantuan animal sculptures surrounding the rubber turf.

Towering parrots with their wings out wide. A rabbit on all fours with its ears flopped down to the dirt. A wavy snake that weaves in and out of the grass with a gaped mouth that children can climb inside.

By day, the park is a playdate daydream. Now, under the light of a nearly full moon, a few dim streetlamps, and the not-so-distant floodlights of Carson Tennis Club, the animals are less like statues and more like sentinels. If the sculptures are really guarding the playground after dark, they're doing a poor job. After all, Kit Park houses a Hackley kickback for different cliques several nights a week. Even on a random Thursday night like tonight.

Caris and I step off the sidewalk and into the hushed laughter of high schoolers with nowhere else to go. A handful of juniors and seniors sit in a semicircle around a half-empty pack of hard seltzers like a bonfire with no fire. The pungent smell of weed wafts from a shadowed crew burrowed beneath a blanket under the slide. Some freshmen with older siblings have taken cover beneath the monkey bars, passing a vape pen between the three of them. Tucked into the tire swing with obnoxious intimacy, Brad hands Jasmine a can of hard seltzer from the inside pocket of his varsity jacket. I guess they've reached a truce in the pursuit of prom king and queen.

We join the semicircle, and I accept a drink from one of Brad's friends. His name is Cameron, and I'm pretty sure he's the one that's good enough on the field to earn a full ride to college. He's also the only Black footballer on the team. So, in typical San Diego suburban fashion, that means our dads know each other.

"How's it going, Ashly?" he says.

I crack open the can. "Ask me again after I finish this. I bet you'll get a better answer."

Cameron chuckles. One of the junior girls offers a seltzer to Caris, who shakes her head and pulls out a flask of her own.

The girl looks crestfallen, which means she probably wanted Caris's attention more than anything.

"Aren't flasks for old men?" the girl tries, her tone flirty.

Caris couldn't care less. She tilts her head back, taking a long swig of whatever organic concoction she's brought. Her silver necklace with the Dara knot pendant flashes against her throat, and even after she's done with her drink, she keeps her eyes on the stars. For someone who practically begged me to go out tonight, she's doing a good job of ignoring everything. Or maybe nothing interesting enough has happened yet to captivate her.

As if on cue, Brad hops out of the tire swing. "Hey!" Jasmine says, as the swing teeters dangerously. She barely keeps her drink off her shirt.

"Sorry, babe," he says. "Just gonna grab some smoke."

Brad crosses the monkey bars, where his little brother shoves him on the shoulder. Rolling his eyes, he continues toward the slide, which means he has to pass our semicircle. His Birkenstocked feet lead him directly to me. I'm not surprised.

"I didn't know you were here, Ash," he says. There's a slight slur in his words, and he's using the nickname I've never liked. All the signs point to him being one of the first to arrive this evening.

"Next time, I'll announce my arrival."

Brad smiles sloppily. "I wouldn't mind that." He kneels to where I'm sitting. I turn away, feigning a drink of hard seltzer. Unfortunately, Cameron is to my right, and he thinks I'm giving him a Brad-and-I-need-privacy look. So, it's just me and Brad, face-to-face, now. Caris is nearby, but history foretells that she won't be intervening unless our conversation turns ugly.

"I'm here," I say flatly.

"Remember freshman year?"

This takes me a bit by surprise. "What about it?"

"It was my first game for Hackley. I was just on JV back then. We were tied. The ball was in my hands, and the receiver was in the perfect position for a touchdown."

Apparently, tonight's alcohol is making a storyteller out of Brad. I grimace as he blathers on. "Everything was clear, but then—it was weird. I felt this tap on my back, and like an idiot, I looked over my shoulder. One split second of distraction, and then I was tackled down. It cost us the game in the end."

Football is a surefire way to bore me, but Brad's story hits a nerve. I remember that day, too. I saw what tapped him. A small flock of pixies had been darting through the game that whole night. Brad's chance to secure a win was exactly the kind of opportunity that any mischievous faerie loved to take advantage of. His loss stirred up a trill of giggles from the pixies.

"Coach chewed me out," Brad says. "All my teammates were pissed. That was the worst post-game locker room moment of my life. When we came back out, no one would talk to me. But you walked right up to me. You said, *Good game*. I heard the next day that you'd been kicked off tennis earlier that week. I felt like we were in the same boat."

It would seem the alcohol is also making him more honest. "Are you complimenting me right now?" I say.

He shrugs. "You play hard, but at least you always say what you mean."

"Hey, Brad," Cameron calls from under the slide. "You coming over or what?"

"Duty calls," Brad says to me. He stands and tips his can toward me. "Cheers, Harris."

I tap my can tentatively against his. When he finally leaves, I breathe a sigh of relief. Brad and I are not friends. Any niceties he's tossed my way are generally followed by a come-on. If Cameron hadn't interrupted, Brad would have probably ruined his sweet talk by hitting on me right in front of Jasmine.

But his words almost sting. Saying what I really mean has never gotten me anywhere. So what if I managed to cheer Brad up? That's one blip in a lifetime of being shut down. *Be quiet. Be good.* Don't be Ashly. I watch Brad join his circle of friends. What would it be like to have a whole circle of friends?

I glance over to Jasmine and nearly choke on my seltzer when our eyes meet. She's glaring daggers my way. Two regrettable hookups with Brad over the course of my high school career evidently make us mortal enemies. I'm trying to decide whether to flip her off when the shadows cast by the tire swing shift into a sinister shape. No amount of blinking or head shaking clears my vision. Long dark hair, black feathers, ice cold eyes, and blue skin. Raven is back.

She hovers over Jasmine, who has started fiddling with her phone. As Jasmine text-vents to her friends, she has no idea that Raven is peering over her shoulder. A sneer cuts into the dark elf's features.

"Raven is over there," I say just loud enough for Caris to hear. No doubt she also picks up on the tremble in my voice because she glances up immediately.

Caris follows my gaze straight to the tire swing. "And what does she think she's doing?"

"Stalking Jasmine for no good reason. Why would Raven give Jasmine the time of day?"

"Why does anyone give Jasmine the time of day?" Caris sizes Jasmine up with a slightly belligerent expression. Jasmine's long legs are crossed over the edge of the tire swing. Her dark hair is pulled into a seamless ponytail, and her red lips are pursed in a perfect pout.

"What, are you checking out Jasmine Bennett now?" I say, and even I realize how unnecessarily spiteful that sounds.

"As if she's worth my time." Still, Caris lingers on Jasmine. I tell myself she's looking for the faerie, but that makes no sense. The seltzer must be going to my head.

So, I pull out my phone, distracting myself with more Google searches about faeries. The keywords *dark elf* and *stalking* lead me to an obscure page reminiscent of nineties' internet blogs.

"Check this out," I say, which finally manages to pull Caris away from Jasmine. "This site mentions something about dark elves specializing in black magic."

Caris laughs. "What is black magic?"

"Don't ask me. It also says that they're experts in espionage, possession, and assassination."

She tsks. "Like I said, don't get involved."

"Well, I'm not about to watch a goth faerie go on a killing spree at Kit Playground."

I gulp down the rest of my drink and head toward Jasmine, completely unsure of what I'm supposed to do to scare off an assassin elf. I doubt *shoo* would work. So, I stick around the freshmen beneath the monkey bars and try to come up with a plan.

Raven walks in circles around the tire swing, shoving her face into Jasmine's phone screen or imperceptibly picking up the ends of her ponytail. To eyes that can't see her, Raven could just be a persistent wind. The feathers on her shoulders look pointed and sharp in the moonlight. A faerie fawning over a human is a rare sight and, in my experience, nothing more than a curse.

One of the freshmen, Brad's brother, tries to pass me the vape, but I wave it away. Short of stomping over and shoving Raven off, I have no idea what to do.

Unfortunately, Jasmine takes note of my stares. She pockets her phone and jumps off the swing. She huffs toward me, and we meet beneath the monkey bars.

"Just leave me alone," Jasmine says as she walks past me.

The freshmen stop vaping, sensing that something interesting is about to go down. Through it all, Raven never lets Jasmine out of her sight.

"Hey," I say, as my brain desperately tries to cook up something more to tell her other than, *There's a dark elf that's got it out for you.* Still, it's enough to make Jasmine halt in her tracks.

"What on earth would I have to say to you right now?" she snaps.

Her snarkiness feels especially sharp, considering I'm trying to help her. That's got me questioning why I'm trying to help someone who I can't stand. But I remember our doubles back in middle school, or even the time in fifth grade when she dashed into our classroom to show off her new Hello Kitty backpack.

"Didn't we used to be friends?" I finally say. I guess Brad's sentimental speech from earlier rubbed off on me, along with the seltzer.

"Then lay off my boyfriend." With that, Jasmine prances over to the slide. Brad puts an arm around her, and I'm left dazed and wishing I hadn't said anything at all.

To make matters worse, Raven has her icy gaze fixed on me now. The last thing I need is another altercation like the one I had with Wolf at the tennis court. Raven lifts her fingers to her lips before dragging a needlelike nail across her tongue.

Goose bumps break out along my skin. How am I supposed to fight off Raven in front of Jasmine, Brad, and everyone else?

"I used to play on these as a kid all the time."

I startle as the junior girl that tried to drink with Caris sneaks up on me from behind. She probably approached just like any other normal person, but I'm on edge and more than a little surprised that she would talk to me. I recognize her from the varsity tennis team. She has dishwater hair and a rainbow bracelet on her wrist.

"Want some Skittles?" she asks. At first, I think she's talking about drugs, but she actually whips out a red candy bag.

Her smile is shy enough to remind me that I haven't hooked up with anyone since fall break. Not that I've made any attempts either.

"Sure," I say, holding out my hand. As she pours a few candies into my palm, I steal a glance toward the tire swing. No Raven. Before I can breathe a sigh of relief, a shadow shifts near the oversized parrot sculpture. Ice blue eyes pierce me. I knock back the candy, faking nonchalance.

"My name's Iris by the way," the junior girl says, completely oblivious.

I'm ninety percent certain that Iris already knows my name. The fact that she's even introduced herself is pretty strange. Most tennis players steer clear of me because they're too afraid of my bad reputation. After all, according to my Hackley reputation, I'm an unreliable party girl with mood swings, and a homewrecking queen. I can at least refute the second accusation.

Iris gulps down a handful of Skittles. "Do you think Caris would want some?"

So, that's the game she's playing at. Iris is fishing for intel on Caris, and I'm stuck in the middle of her flirtation. Not to mention the dark elf is still haunting us a few yards away.

"Caris is more of a natural, raw sugars kind of girl," I say. The faerie still hasn't moved from the parrot sculpture.

"Oh, does she like chocolate, then?"

I roll my eyes, not wanting to get into a science lesson. Unless Iris is packing some unrefined cacao in her pocket, she'd better give up before she gets started. Apparently, even Raven thinks chocolate conversations are too boring for any tricks because she slinks away. If I didn't know any better,

Raven would be nothing but a shadow slipping behind the parrot sculpture's wings. Then there's nothing more than a breeze murmuring through the trees.

"There's different kinds of sugar," I say, feeling more generous now that Raven is gone. "She's a sweetened-with-maple-syrup kind of person, not a candy or chocolate person."

"So, are you two dating? You're always together."

Still lounging at the semicircle, Caris has lain down on her back. She's got her eyes on the stars again. Since elementary school, Caris never seemed to need any friends other than me. Everyone likes her. Or more like no one hates her. She's the wind on a hot day, always welcome but uncatchable.

"I'm not sure if Caris dates," I say honestly.

Iris laughs. "At least she's not unavailable."

Part of me wants to object, but I squash that as quick as I can. For all the random guys and girls I've kissed, I can't be undermining Caris's chances with anyone. Besides, she and I are friends, and friends don't get jealous like that.

But I don't have to play matchmaker either. "Thanks for the Skittles," I say.

When I head back toward the seltzers, Iris stays for a hit off the freshman's vape. The freshmen watch me as I walk away. Tonight could have been better. It could have been me and Caris, holed up in my bedroom, stealing drinks from her flask and pretending like graduation isn't only a few months away. I'm not a freak when it's just the two of us. And Caris would say that freaks have more fun anyway.

When I finally take my place at Caris's side, she rolls over.

"Raven is gone," I tell her, but she shrugs like she already knew or doesn't really care.

"I didn't realize that Iris was your type," she says.

I shake my head. "I think she's trying to figure out if she's your type."

"My type?" Caris sits up. "I have higher standards."

Iris is cute. She's got a pretty face and a tennis player's

body. Apparently, she can hang out with seniors and freshmen, and no one seems to be cutting glares in her direction. "How high?" I ask.

"That girl can't even see faeries," Caris says. "I don't walk home any girls who can't see faeries."

CHAPTER EIGHT

The TV casts an eerie glow across the dark living room, illuminating the silhouettes of the furniture, the picture frames, and, of course, my dad. He's sitting on the couch as a sitcom rerun flickers across the whites of his eyes.

I expected my parents would wait up for me once they realized I wasn't home tonight. Still, I'm wondering why Mom isn't sitting beside him. Unless, of course, she's given up on me by now.

My sneakers scuff on the rug. The expression on Dad's face as he sizes me up is less like anger and more like exhaustion. I prefer anger. It's easier to tune out. After all, no one can hold a candle to my own anger.

Resigned to my fate, I take a seat on the fraying fabric of the gray couch. One of the sofa pillows rests on the floor. It must have fallen sometime during the evening. I hug it to my chest and run my fingers along its plaid embroidery. That's when I realize I'm upset or nervous or some other unhappy feeling. The pillow hug was an old trick my therapist taught me to calm down. I had a bad habit of yelling in our sessions, or anytime I got upset. I still do. I've just gotten better at caring less, so I don't wind up shouting anymore, most of the time.

"You wanna watch this?" Dad asks. I shake my head. I'm not a fan of TV comedies. My parents and I don't have the kind of relationship where we sit on the couch and laugh at movies together. I might be able to find a memory or two of fun family times, but that was before the faeries took center stage. Dad shuts off the TV, which throws us into pitch-black darkness before he clicks on the lamp beside him.

"I've been thinking about what to say to you when you finally came home," he continues. "During commercial breaks, at least."

I smile weakly. "What did you decide on?"

"Your mom and I talked about it, too. She'll talk to you over breakfast tomorrow. I don't know if you remember this, but she's interviewing for her promotion tomorrow."

I totally forgot. "Good thing she went to bed," I say, biting back the guilt. Mom and Dad work a lot of overtime. All for larger paychecks, I guess. Tennis lessons aren't cheap. Kids aren't cheap in general, but they're burning money on my future. Each failing grade and phone call home is evidence that I'm a bad investment. I dig my nails into the pillow to keep from throwing it back on the floor. I never signed up to be someone's investment.

"Well, you've been dealing with your own problems," Dad says. "Senior year is a weird time. Everyone's trying to pretend they're already in college, but they have no idea what it's like to be on their own. College is a lot better. Less petty."

Dad left San Diego for an HBU in Alabama, then wound up back in California for another historically Black graduate school in Los Angeles. The twist in the story is how he met my mom in grad school. My dad gets asked all the time, *If you went to an HBU, how did you meet Annie?* I guess people don't know that the US Constitution makes it so that no institution can discriminate based on race, and that nurses like my mom, who was looking to leave Arizona, might apply to private schools across California, including HBUs.

I also guess people don't know that it's rude to ask invasive questions just because a couple is mixed race. *Is he your stepdad? Are you adopted? You don't look like either of your parents.* The list goes on. Making new friends is pretty hard when people keep staring at me sideways before asking, *What* are *you?* That's a great question to have hanging over my head twenty-four seven, and no one has signed up to help me figure out how to answer it.

"College sounds like a blast," I say.

"You can do this, Ashly. Even if you don't realize it, you can. Since you were little, you've been chasing after big things. You're so fast, you forget to slow down and do the busywork."

"Like going to bed at a decent time and following the rules and not hanging out with…" I pause on the word *friends* because the Kit Playground crew doesn't quite fit the bill. "And not hanging out when I'm supposed to be grounded?"

"Like going to class and doing your homework and taking pointers from Lanie," he says gently.

We've finally come to the real subject of our little chat. A fuse sparks to life in my chest. I jump off the couch and book it to the open kitchen, so I won't blow up. Dad watches me the whole way, like a patient trainer with a skittish dog. I wish he would get mad, ground me an extra month, and send me to my room. The heart-to-heart tactic doesn't work when your daughter can't tell you about her problems without landing her in a psychologist's office the next day.

Containers of leftovers, diced meal prep, and four-day-old cookies line the refrigerator shelves. I grab a cookie and pour myself a glass of vanilla almond milk. After a bite and a long gulp of milk, I thunk the glass on the counter and cast Dad a look that I hope will end this conversation for the night.

He sighs and unfortunately walks into the kitchen. After grabbing his own cookie, he leans against the counter. Mom would be mad we aren't using plates.

"You've got a lot of people in your corner, Ashly, whether you realize it or not. There's me, your mom, and Lanie. Some of your teachers send us emails with concerns, too. We all want you to succeed—to make progress."

I grab two plates from the cabinet so I don't have to look him in the eye. Of course, they all want me to do better, to be different, but I don't know how to make any progress in unseeing faeries. Not to mention that the faeries have their own goals. It just so happens that their goals involve making a mess out of whatever success I manage to dredge up.

"Maybe a change of scenery will do you good in the end," he says.

My stomach drops. "What is that supposed to mean?"

"Mom told you about Grandma, right? Her burn is healing well, but we're still really concerned about her living by herself. She's stubborn and doesn't want any help unless it comes from family. Your Aunt Erin has been calling more frequently. She's not doing all right. Managing a career, your cousins, and Grandma—she needs help."

"Sounds really bad," I say, because it does. Aunt Erin is tough as nails, so if she needs help, the situation must be serious.

"So, Mom and I have been talking about moving to Phoenix this summer. My company is willing to keep me on remotely. Your mom is a nurse. She can go anywhere."

"But Mom's promotion," I say.

Dad nods. "Nothing is set in stone, but wherever we go, you can come with us."

"What if I don't want to go?" I care about Grandma. I wouldn't mind another summer with her. Even though she's sick and a little foggy, her laughter has always been warm and her smiles full of secret whispers. As a little kid, she would wink at me if she caught me scolding faeries in the backyard. I want her to live a long life, as long as possible.

But leaving San Diego is something I don't want either.

"To be honest, I didn't realize you like it that much here," Dad says. "A fresh start in a new place could be a reset for you. Right now, you don't have any plans for college or vocational school. At least a move to Phoenix is something."

Dad's right. I don't have any plans lined up for after graduation. I'm still not sure about graduation itself, but I have Caris here. We have our midnight chats and spontaneous adventures. She somehow shows up when I need her, without a text or a call. That's something worth holding on to. She's not someone I could replace in Arizona.

"I can get a job here," I say.

Dad shakes his head. "It's not just a job, Ashly. It's whether you can pay rent on a place by yourself."

"I have Caris."

"Is Caris staying and working here?"

A heavy sigh escapes my chest. "She won't say. She might be going to college, but she hasn't actually told me if she's been admitted or accepted or to where."

"Well, if she isn't going to college and is planning to stay here, she would have probably told you by now, right? That way, you two could work out some next steps."

Just like that, Dad has reached into my heart, yanked out my worst fear, and laid it on the kitchen counter, all with a side of plain logic and straightforward sense. Caris is going away. The fact that she hasn't told me where is only proof that I won't be a part of her future.

"You always have a place with us," Dad says as he clanks his plate in the sink. "Think about it."

I stare blankly as Dad drags his tired feet across the living room. Before he ducks into the hall, he mutters a simple good night. My parents' bedroom door creaks shut, and my head is spinning.

Without a solid post-graduation plan, I have no choice but to move to Phoenix. Even if I drew up a chart, with a life in Arizona on one side and one in San Diego on the other, the difference between the two is slim. I'll be facing each day by myself no matter where I go.

CHAPTER NINE

The next several days feel like walking on a battered bridge between two clifftops. As promised, Mom had lectured me pitilessly in the morning. She and Dad must have been playing good cop, bad cop with me. Or Grandma's health has really stretched Mom thin. They switch roles back and forth for a week, so I never feel quite safe with either of them. Let's just say I'm glad it's Friday.

At least that's how I felt till my government teacher served us a ten-page review packet with content I feel like I'm learning for the first time. When I finally arrive at the tennis club for after-school practice, I shove my government textbook into my locker. That's a small improvement—at least I'm bringing the textbook home.

February may be about to end, but this is California, so even though I'm cold out of my mind, I'm still supposed to play on an outdoor court. I shuffle on my leggings, tank, jacket, and sneakers and prepare for a practice that promises to be more like torture than tennis drills. Then I recall once more that it's Friday, and what was it that Jasmine Bennett said last week? She's getting private lessons on Fridays now.

Too nosy to care about invasion of privacy, I trail my fingers to the locker that Jasmine used back in middle school. No lock, of course. I pop it open, and sure enough her pink gym bag and designer Mary Janes are stuffed inside. My stomach squeezes. At least I avoided a hostile locker room exchange.

I'm a bit early to practice again, but I figure I can warm up on the court if Lanie hasn't arrived yet. I step out of the locker room, into the corridor, and right into Caris. In all our years of friendship, Caris has never once met me at the tennis club. I'm pretty sure my eyes bulge out of my face to epic proportions.

"What are you doing here?" I practically shout.

A sardonic grin pulls at her lips. "What? I can't come see you when I want to?"

"Oh, whatever, like you've ever come to the tennis club. To what do I owe this great honor, your majesty?" I fake a bow, and Caris barks out a laugh.

"I could get used to this," she says, sort of sharply, which knocks the wind out of my sails. Something is up. I don't know what, but that's too low a sarcastic blow, even for Caris.

Maybe she's finally about to tell me the truth: *She's leaving me for good after graduation.*

I take my place beside her against the wall, grateful for the few minutes I have to waste before practice. She seems content to let the silence linger, but I'm not about to play docile. "So, did you decide on a college yet?" I say.

Caris shrugs. "I'm not sure about that."

"Oh." She's not going to make this easy. "Then you have a few you're considering?"

"What about you?"

"What do you mean? You know I didn't apply anywhere." I sigh. "I guess there's community college, or I can try to get some work."

My Dad's word's ring in my ears. *It's not just a job, Ashly. It's whether you can pay rent on a place by yourself.* By now I should've told Caris about Arizona. After all, I could be moving in T-minus four months. We won't even be able to watch the Kit Park Fourth of July fireworks together, ditching our parents, holed up together in whatever private corner we can find. But If Caris plans to dodge the college talk, then I don't owe her anything.

In the middle of our uncomfortable silence, Caris cracks her neck. Her necklace gleams beneath the ceiling lights. For the first time in ten years, the pendant is different. Instead of a Dara knot, there's a large tree, much like the Celtic tree of life but upside-down, etched into the silver.

"Check it out," I say. "You swapped your pendant. I didn't even know you had another one."

"Change is good," Caris says, then takes out a store-bought chocolate bar from her jacket pocket. She breaks off a block and swallows.

"Whoa there! You're eating regular chocolate?"

She shrugs again. "It tastes decent. Want some?"

As Caris drops a piece in my hand, my mind buzzes with questions. Caris seems distracted or something. What happened to my Caris, and how do I kick the normal version back into gear? I guess I'm not the only one stressed about graduation.

The chocolate is sweeter than any I've ever tasted, almost like pure sugar but with a tart aftertaste. The block melts on my tongue faster than ice in an oven. I guess if Caris would choose a conventional chocolate, this would be the bar to die for.

I glance at the clock near the exit. One minute till I'm late to practice. "Thanks for stopping by for once," I say. "Gotta head out."

As I head toward the door, a shadow snags at the corner of my vision. For a breath, I see a flash of red eyes in place of Caris's brown. Then it's gone, and Caris is Caris. A wave of dizziness hits me, and now I'm wondering if the stress is finally getting to me. I'm cracking, seeing things for real this time. My stomach does a somersault. An eye color change is abnormal, even for me.

But I've still got practice.

"I'll see you later," Caris says.

I trip on my feet out the door, half wondering why Caris is still in the corridor. The other part of me is questioning why I'm so affected by her strange mood. It's got me so messed up that I can't see straight. I clear a few deep breaths. In the distance, I hear the thwack of a volley on the court in the distance. Jasmine must be acing her private lesson.

I step onto my practice court, and the gate crashes shut behind me. Lanie is dribbling a ball on the opposite side of the net. I was supposed to be early, but at least I'm here now and still on time. That has to count for something.

Lanie throws some small talk my way, and I fumble through. The dizziness is still surging through me. Lanie must notice my struggle because she leaves her side of the court for mine.

"Let's start with some two-ball tosses," she says.

Sounds like child's play to me, but my breath swirls in my ears. Fire flares in my arms and legs. Lanie pulls two balls out of her pockets, then stands about two yards from me. She lifts her left leg and tosses me the first ball. I lift mine, balancing with all my might, and catch the ball. Easy.

Except now we have to stay like this, balancing, catching, and throwing a ball at each other at the same time. My head starts to ache, and my ankle shudders. Just a few tosses in and I'm back on two feet, breathing heavily.

Lanie shakes her head. She throws her ball, but I see three balls flying toward me. My right hand fails to catch any of them. My left hand is still holding on to the ball that I never managed to toss. I'm barely able to stay standing.

"Give me a second," I say.

"You've gotta be kidding me, Ashly." Lanie follows me as I stumble to the chain-link fence. "What's the excuse now? What reason do you have today for wasting our time?"

I cram my eyes shut. "I feel nauseous."

"I wouldn't be surprised if you're drunk. Did you come to practice intoxicated?"

The chain-link fence bends beneath my weight. My fingers squeeze the metal, not because I can't stand on my own, but because I'm pissed. "You really think I'd do that?" I ask Lanie. Shoving down the hurt, I lace my words with anger.

"What am I supposed to think, Ashly? Wake up. Look around yourself, and then look at yourself. I used to think it was just some kind of phase or an act, but you seem bent on becoming as much of a bad girl as you possibly can."

I push myself off the fence. Lanie is the same height as me. Head-to-head. "You think this is bad," I say. "I could be so much worse. Go ahead and call my parents about this. I bet they're expecting it."

Lanie doesn't even call me back. I resist the urge to glance over my shoulder. She could be furious or disappointed or sorry. Or she might be staring me down with a face full of indifference. My heart broils stronger with each of my shaky steps forward. I feel the whisper of unspoken words at my back: *You're a lost cause, Ashly.* I'm a burning building. If the fire rages on, soon I'll be nothing but a pile of ash.

I stumble down the corridor and reach the locker room, sick to my stomach, holding the wall for support. Shadows creep into my vision, and I blink hard to fight them back. Rage and frustration swirl through me, but I don't know how to fight against that. All I need to do is grab my belongings from my locker and call an Uber. Once I get home, I can throw up and pass out, or whatever it is that my body is begging me to do.

Except Jasmine Bennett is standing in front of her locker, gleaming with post-practice sweat. I wish I could push past her, bash her locker door shut with a bang, *anything*, but instead, I collapse against the tile wall and slide down to the cold floor. The bright lights stab my throbbing eyes.

Jasmine kneels in front of me, but there's no concern

written on her face. I want her to back off. I want to shove her away with the palm of my hand.

"How the mighty have fallen," she says.

Her words hit like a skinned knee on gravel. While I wish I could punch her perfect nose, my leaden arms stay pinned to the floor. A memory worms into my mind: *Ten-year-old me, lying exhausted in a sleeping bag after a fun day with my tennis team. Jasmine slept across from me, her pink sleeping bag tucked beneath her chin. "Ashly," she whispered, "you played really good today. I want to be as good as you someday."*

"You are as good as me," I whispered back, eyes still closed.

"Then," she said so softly I almost didn't hear her, "I want to be better."

I hear Jasmine slam her locker shut. She saunters out without another glance my way. If she's anything like the old Jasmine Bennett, the one I used to play with, she's left a backup bag of tennis gear in her locker. Hatred twists in my gut, and I wonder what it would be like to throw all of her things in the shower, just like the faerie did when we were in the seventh grade.

Maybe it's time for me to stop resisting all the faerie mischief. I could embrace it. I could enjoy it.

I sigh, lifting myself off the floor with what little strength I have left. Even with my razor-sharp tongue and hard-as-nails attitude, I don't have it in me to trash other people's gear. I just want to go home.

My breath floods my ears as I drag my feet to my locker. I snap open the locker door. I can do this. I reach for my bag. Halfway there. Then the shadows swarm my sight until everything is black. My breathing is louder than a storm.

And then, there's nothing.

❖

Water trickles down my face. I sputter, then cough. It's cold. I'm cold, and my eyes sting as I blink them open. My body aches. I'm being weighed down, and when I finally lift my head, I see a pink tennis racket, clothes, and a tennis bag that looks a lot like Jasmine's.

A throat clears, and even though I have no idea how I ended up in the shower with Jasmine's stuff all over me, I don't have time to figure it out, because I'm not alone. Not by a longshot.

Lanie hovers over me with crossed arms and a frown deep enough to cut permanent lines in her skin. Beside her are a few familiar faces that I can't quite place. Their crisp uniforms tell me that they work at the tennis club.

"You said she might be intoxicated?" one of the club managers asks Lanie. "Didn't she do something like this with people's tennis gear a few years ago?"

I want to scream no, that I was just feeling inexplicably sick. That I've never thrown anyone's gear in the shower. That was the faerie. It's always the faeries.

Instead, I stare into Lanie's eyes, begging her to stick up for me, to take my side this one time.

Lanie just shakes her head. "Ashly, you've really thrown it all away."

CHAPTER TEN

I'm disqualified indefinitely from tennis. The evidence against me was too incriminating, and no one believed that I'd been set up. Lanie told them all what a wreck I'd been during practice, how I'd rampaged my way off the court. It's not like I could blame the faeries, especially with Jasmine's gear in the shower. My parents hired Lanie because I was willing to lie about the faeries. Now I've lost her to the charade.

I'd like to say it could be worse, but I'm not sure how much lower I can go. Where does the deep end hit bottom? I've lost tennis, I'm grounded till I manage to make it on my own, and I'm slated to fail school. Curling up in a fetal position on my bed feels like my only option.

What I need most is for someone to tell me that everything will somehow be all right. In other words, I want Caris. But I can't text her or call her. Short of opening my window and calling out into the night, I have no way to contact her. She only turns up when she wants to, like at the tennis club earlier this afternoon. Right before I tripped out of purgatory and straight into hell.

Apparently, a full evening of telling me to be a better person makes my parents knock-out tired. Good for them. I'm stuck staying up past whatever a godly hour is, watching my walls in the hopes that something moves. In my room, I'm the only living thing, and that makes me lonelier than anything.

I'm always at a standstill, except on the court, but now the court is beyond my reach.

To be honest, I don't know if I trashed Jasmine's things or if the faeries did. There was no one else in the locker room. Only me and my blind rage. That just about sums up my life. Sadly, it doesn't actually matter if faeries destroy the world, starting with Carson Tennis Club. When you're the only one who sees the catastrophes for what they are, then you might as well jump headfirst into the pandemonium.

My home is so silent that it's unbearable. I peel myself from my bed and go to the window. No Caris in sight. After yanking the window up, I breathe in the cool night air. Mom and Dad have grounded me till graduation. Considering that my graduation is a major toss-up, I shrug off their punishment and stick one foot out the window. The cold wind greets my ankle with a frigid hello. Before I can question my choices, I swing two legs over. Freedom breathes a breeze over my face.

In nothing but an oversize T-shirt and dolphin shorts, I hop off the windowsill. The dewy grass hits my bare feet. I let my steps carry me around the front of the house to the backyard gate. The lock clanks as I unlatch it, and the gate groans loudly. If my parents somehow heard the sound in their sleep, I figure there are worse things they could catch me doing than visiting the backyard at midnight. Their biggest question would revolve around my choice to enter through the gate instead of our sliding glass door. I don't have an answer for that.

The automatic porch light switches on, illuminating the garden that my parents maintain together. Small plots of kale and spinach rest safely behind wire barricades to keep the rabbits out. I pass beneath a lemon tree, its sour oily scent wafting by. Finally, I settle beside the hellebores, which is a fancy name for what my parents also refer to as *winter roses*.

The grass itches my leg, and another breeze sifts through my hair, raising goose bumps on my neck. Everything should be quiet, and any normal person would feel peacefully asleep, yet I hear a tinkling of laughter from the hellebores. Leaning over, I spy a tiny pixie curled up in the center of one of the flowers. A pink petal covers half her body, like a blanket, but her black eyes are wide open, blinking brightly in my direction.

"Hello," I say.

She giggles again, then yawns. Pillowing her head on her small arms, she closes her eyes and drifts to sleep.

When I was little, the faeries I saw were almost always like this. They were simple, sweet even. Faeries were magical. Life was an adventure. It was fun.

The sound of shuffling footsteps creeps up behind me. I turn, expecting Dad or Mom, or another faerie, but it's Caris.

"Your window was open," she says before taking a seat beside me.

"I was feeling a little claustrophobic, so I came out here. Today has sucked, and that's putting it lightly."

"What makes this day worse than other days?"

It's true. Ever since this semester started, I've been barely keeping my head above the burden of getting out of bed. My shoulders feel like they're sagging lower and lower, the pressure sinking me down somewhere between graduation and old tennis rivalries, with faeries pushing me beneath the surface whenever I try to come up for air.

"I'm done with tennis forever," I say. "Or more like, tennis is done with me. I got sick at practice, and Lanie thought I was drunk. Then I blacked out in the locker room and woke up in the shower. Somehow, all of Jasmine's gear wound up on top of me, and now everyone thinks I had some kind of meltdown. How's that for worse than normal?"

Caris leans on her elbows, which might come off as apathetic, except for the way her eyebrows knit together. "How did you wind up showering with Jasmine's tennis gear?"

"Maybe I did it in a blacked-out fit of fury. Who knows?"

The motion-sensor porchlight switches off suddenly, so I

can't make out Caris's face anymore in the darkness. I wave my arms until it clicks back on. The light glints off Caris's necklace.

"Oh, you changed your necklace back," I say. I'm tired of talking about faeries and the mess that makes up my life.

"What does that mean?" Caris asks as she fingers the Dara knot pendant hanging from the silver chain around her neck.

"When you came to the tennis club earlier, your pendant was an upside-down tree. Did you get a new one when you were in Hawaii?"

"Ashly, I've never been to that tennis club," Caris says in a voice low enough to sound almost like a warning. "Not once in all the years we've known each other."

"I know, so I'm not gonna lie, it kind of weirded me out when you showed up today. That chocolate was pretty good, though. I could use another bite if you have any left. Something sweet to take the edge off this shitty day."

In the blink of an eye, Caris grabs my wrist. Shocked, I instinctively pull away, but she grasps me more tightly. "I wasn't at the tennis club today, Ashly."

My heart crashes to the pit of my stomach. I could argue. I could recount to Caris all the things she said in the locker room corridor. I could beg her to tell me that she was there, but the truth is easier to accept for once. I've finally tipped over the edge of whatever precipice I've been teetering on. There have always been excuses for why I can see faeries when no one else can, but there is no excuse or explanation for hallucinating Caris.

I groan and squint my eyes shut, blocking out the world. I cover them for good measure. "I can't do this anymore. I've finally cracked, huh? I know what you're thinking: I'm not special. I don't have some kind of supernatural power. There's no such thing as the Sight."

Caris shifts closer to me until our knees touch. Her hand

still holds my wrist tightly. "C'mon, Ashly. There's all that stuff online about the Sight. Lots of people have it."

"There's no evidence. A bunch of weirdos on a forum playing pretend doesn't make me less of a freak."

"You're not a freak." Caris tugs me upward, so we're both standing. The softness in her eyes makes me want to believe her. "Come with me. Let's get out of here."

"I'm grounded for life."

"Who cares if we get caught, then? It's not like your parents can add another day to a life sentence."

There's no arguing with that logic. I let Caris lead me away from the garden and out the backyard gate. We trudge through the grass to the chain-link fence we jumped a few weeks earlier. I'm not wearing any shoes, but I follow Caris over the fence. For once, I don't care about the mud squelching between my toes.

A stick snaps beneath Caris's lace-up boots. After a branch slashes my arm, she stops and shrugs off her buttonless jean jacket. My heart skips when she gently places it across my shoulders. This is a different Caris. The dry humor has evaporated, and something else has taken its place. Something tender. A Caris that no one else has witnessed but me.

Not too long after, we emerge from the trees into a clearing. A crescent moon winks at us from the sky, encircled by the tops of the trees. In the night light, I make out the grassy hill where we shared the picnic. Caris steps forward, but when I try to join her, she shakes her head.

Slowly, as though stirred by our presence, the faeries appear from behind the tree trunks. Unlike last time, an assortment of creatures come out to greet us. Their beady eyes stare us down. Or more specifically, they all seem to stare straight at Caris.

Caris turns to the left. "Dwarfs," she says to the short-statured men perched on an oak's roots.

She turns to the right. "Sprites," she says to two female fae with glittering wings.

She looks to the top of the hill toward a cloud of glowing orbs. "Pixies."

I can hardly breathe. As if called by Caris, the faeries draw closer. The wind stirs her hair, and her eyes hold the light of the moon.

Suddenly, I take in all the details, the ones I've individually noticed but can now piece together into the full picture. The missing buttons in her jacket because the iron would burn her skin. Never using a cell phone, hating cars and airplanes. Her disgust for artificial flavors. The Celtic knot on her necklace. Her enchanting ability to command so much attention and yet never stir up any trouble.

"You're one of them," I whisper.

Without realizing it, I've made my way to Caris. Her lips curve into a soft smile, but my heart is racing. I'm not sure if I've lost my closest friend or if I'm finally meeting her for the first time. Seeing her for who she really is for the very first time.

Her hand grazes my cheek, then rests beneath my chin. "It's about time you figured it out," she says.

"But you're human. I've known you since we were kids. How come I didn't know?"

With her free hand, she taps the pendant around her neck. "There are ways to hide that even the Sight can't see through."

"I wish you had told me. Why didn't you?"

"I've always wanted to tell you, and now, here we are."

I part my mouth to respond, and Caris traces her thumb over my bottom lip. I've been in this position before. I know all the telltale signs of an oncoming kiss, but I can hardly wrap my mind around the fact that it's Caris. That Caris is a faerie. That this faerie wants to kiss me.

But I don't need to come to terms with the small things

right now. Because I want Caris to kiss me, and I realize now that I've been wanting this for a very long time.

I lean forward, and our lips touch. My eyes flutter shut as my heart dances in my chest. Caris tastes like honey and flowers and well water. Her palms trail down my arm and down my back, sending a thrill of shivers in their wake. I'm holding on to the hem of her tank top, fingers grasping the fabric, as though I could pull her closer than she already is. I want her closer.

But she breaks away, like a whispering wind finally come to rest. Our gazes catch, and for all my doubts about myself and my Sight, I am completely certain that this is true. Caris is a faerie. Somehow, someway, since the day we met. Since forever.

The forest faeries chirr around us, and for the first time in a long time, I am happy that I can see a whole world that no one else can see. A world that Caris sees, too. Caris's world.

CHAPTER ELEVEN

You mean to tell me that you've been lying to me all this time," I say into the rustling night. I can't tell the difference between the wind in the trees and the footfalls of faeries, but I just ignore it. Caris is all I can handle right now. Or, at least, I hope I can handle this.

Caris tsks playfully. "Unlike humans, faeries can't lie, so I haven't been lying to you at all. I may have been hiding the truth."

I vaguely remember learning something about that in a novel I read during my middle school faerie research days. The difference between concealing the truth and lying is vague to say the least. My parents would trample that excuse in two seconds flat.

"Ask me anything," Caris says. "Be specific. You'll see."

With that, Caris spreads her arms out to the sides and falls back on the slanted hill. Lying there, she's an open book, apparently ready to tell me whatever I want to know. I've known Caris for ten years, and I've hardly learned anything about her besides her parents' names, a handful of her dislikes, the way she lightly mocks almost anything that happens, the way she kisses, and the fact that she's a faerie. Those last two are new, and I feel like I might need another month before I can come to terms with them.

Now, Caris says I can ask anything. It's somehow both thrilling and terrifying. I decide to start small.

"Am I crazy?" I blurt, trying to make a joke but sounding a lot more pathetic than I planned. So much for small.

"Much less crazy than the average mortal."

"So, we're all crazy?"

Caris laughs. "Define crazy. I think we may have different definitions."

"Okay," I say, kneeling beside her. "Next question. Are you going to college?"

She sits up and grabs my hips with both her hands. I suck in a breath. "Do you want me to go to college?"

"I thought I was the one asking the questions."

"Of course I'm not going to college."

I cross my arms, feigning indifference to this good news. "Then you're just killing time here with us mortals."

"Since you say so."

"Wow, really?"

"You didn't even ask a question, Ashly," she says, pulling me to the ground. I take a seat next to her, not ready to jump in her lap or whatever my body may be screaming at me to do. "You need to get better at asking questions, or else it's too easy to give you vague answers."

I bristle. "Fine. Are you hanging out with us mortals just to kill time?"

"No comment."

"That's not fair." I wrap my arms around my knees, not caring if I look petulant. "You said you would answer my questions. Then tell me why you've been hanging out at Hackley High School for the last four years. How come I can see all these faeries, but I couldn't see you for what you are?"

Caris considers me closely for a moment. Her gaze is magnetic, drawing me nearer, even though I haven't budged an inch. "I'll tell you everything, but not here. We need neutral ground."

The faeries stir around us. "Where is neutral ground?"

"Let's go back to your room."

We head back the way we came. As we near the edge of the woods, I trip on a shadowed branch, and Caris catches me before I can even curse. She slips her hand in mine and doesn't let go after we start walking again. Sure, my feet are scraped, and blisters are cropping up, but with Caris's fingers tangled in mine, I can't complain. I'm just trying to keep my breath steady.

Finally, we jump the fence and wind up back home. Caris hoists herself through the window first, and I follow.

"Shut the window," she says, as though the faeries would clamber in after us.

Caris takes a seat on my bed, so I sit next to her. We sit there, somewhat awkwardly, until I break the silence. "What's next?"

"Let's start with the basics. I'm a faerie."

"And you never thought to tell me this before. After all these years, you let me think you couldn't so much as see a faerie, and now you're telling me you're one of them."

"Well, not every faerie would be happy to hear me say that I'm fae, since I'm half human."

I curl my legs under me. My knee brushes Caris's thigh, and she doesn't scoot away. "Great," I say casually. "Faerie on faerie discrimination. Sounds a lot like humankind, or like being biracial. Everyone wants you to pick a side, but no one wants you on their side. I know that firsthand."

"It's similar, but completely different. I don't relate to anything that humans say, think, or do. I was raised by the fae for the first seven years of my life. I just look a bit more human than other fae."

"So, are you hiding wings under your tank top?"

Caris grimaces at the thought. "I'm not a sprite or some minor fae. I'm an elf. More specifically, a wood elf."

"Then are elves, like, superior faeries or something?"

She runs a hand through her hair and her eyes flash with amusement. "I can't answer that question without bias."

"This is what you really look like, then?"

"No."

"What do you look like?" I try to imagine her in a new faerie form. The elves I've met recently are the two dark elves with red and ice blue eyes, wearing black fur and raven feathers. Their skin is blue. What color is Caris's true skin?

"I'd have to take off this necklace for you to see me as fae."

"Take it off, then." I say that, but I'm not sure if I'm really ready for a whole new Caris.

She shakes her head. "Let's just say I'd be a little taller than you. Also, my ears would be slightly sharper, my bone structure would be more defined, and my eyes a lot darker."

Given that Caris already has the deepest brown eyes I've ever seen, I'm not sure what darker would look like.

"Then how did those faeries recognize you on the hill?" I ask. "You looked exactly the same, and I've never seen faeries react to you like that before. They never even looked at you."

"I took off some of my glamour, so the woodland fae could sense my power. They were drawn to it, but mere common fae could never recognize me that easily, especially with my pendant sealing their Sight."

The same Sight that I have, the Sight that couldn't see beyond the magic in Caris's pendant. "Your necklace can do more than glamour."

"This is why I like you," she says, turning toward me so that my knee sits in her lap. "Your ancestors must have had dealings with us long ago. You're the only human I've met who can think even slightly like a faerie."

That sounds like a backhanded compliment if I've heard one. "Since you're here, acting like a human, you better play nice."

"Nice is boring." Despite her cocky tone, she trails a hand

down my bare leg. All my nerves stand on end. This would be the perfect moment for a second kiss, but her eyes are distant, looking somewhere beyond me, beyond the four walls of my bedroom.

If the necklace Caris never takes off makes her appear completely human, that explains why she's been able to hide at school, but I can't figure out how Caris's parents took in a random elementary school kid without questioning her origins. I remember an old Celtic tale I came across several years ago. The story described a group of meddling faeries that traded out a baby for a faerie. The human baby was imprisoned in the faerie world, while the faerie tortured its adoptive family for years.

"So, basically, you're a changeling," I say.

Caris scoffs. "Don't use slurs you don't understand."

"I know what a changeling is." It makes sense, after all. Tim and Tina are nothing like Caris. They're simple people who go on holiday vacations and shop for packaged food at our local grocery store. Even if Caris is the best thing that ever happened to me, part of me feels bad knowing that Tim and Tina lost their child to the faeries. "So, where is your parents' real kid?"

"I'm not a changeling."

Caris promised that she can't lie. Still, the idea of Tim and Tina being Caris's birth parents seems even stranger than Caris being a changeling. Caris treats them more like roommates than family. She even calls them by their first names.

"Tim and Tina are simply two mortals who wanted to have a child and couldn't. Thanks to the faeries and a heavy dose of glamour to their memories, they got to experience parenthood for some years."

"Past tense. You make it sound like they're gonna die." A chill goes up my spine. Faeries aren't nice. Nice is boring, right? While I've never seen a faerie kill a human, I'm not naïve enough to think it couldn't happen.

"They'll be fine, but all kids grow up and leave home."

"And go to college," I say.

Caris leans onto the bed. "Like I said before, I'm not going to college."

Her evasive answer tells me something is up. I'm getting the hang of this faeries can't lie thing. "Then where are you going?"

"I'm going home."

Obviously, she doesn't mean back to Tim and Tina's. "Where is home?"

"How about you ask me a better question."

I sigh, growing tired of this game. "Why can't you just tell me the truth straight out?"

"Now, that's a better question," she says, patting my comforter. I curl up beside her. We've lain like this so many times in the past, murmuring in the night. What did we even talk about back then? Our old conversations seem laced with double meanings now that Caris's secret sits between us.

"I never told you these things because I swore not to. An oath is unbreakable for the fae. My true mother sent me here. She gave me the pendant and made me promise to never tell a soul what I am. It's not that I didn't want to tell you. I simply couldn't form the words. My oath froze them to my throat, so I've been waiting for you to realize on your own."

"Your mom sounds like someone I wouldn't want to mess with." My mom couldn't force me to attend all my classes for a week, even if she made me cross my heart and hope to die.

"An oath is an oath, regardless of power. But it's true, you wouldn't want to offend my mother. She is the Queen and far more formidable than the King. Our kingdom is small compared to the two strongest Courts—the Seelie and Unseelie. Our woods border the Seelie and Unseelie kingdoms, which means we get caught up in their affairs more often than we'd like."

I can't help but laugh. "If your parents are Queen and

King, that makes you a princess. Wow, so I've been living in a fairy tale storybook all this time."

Caris frowns. "You're wrong on both accounts. My father isn't King. He's a human, and someone I've never cared to meet. My mother found him during one of her dalliances in the human world. She enjoyed a brief intrigue with him, but humans are rarely deemed worthy of the faerie kingdoms. So, she left him where she found him and gave birth to me in our Court. This sort of thing happens more often than you'd think."

Her confession leaves me with more questions than answers. "Then why did your mom leave you here in the human world?"

"The lives of faeries are hardly like the cute stories you read in elementary school. Faeries never age, which means we kill each other all the time. We wage wars for decades. In the case of my family's Court, we've been caught in the midst of a border conflict with the Seelie and the Unseelie for fifteen years. That's a short war by our standards, but it's been going on for most of my life."

Caris's voice has grown hoarse, but there's no trace of tears in her eyes. She rarely talks about herself, and I wonder if I'm wearing her down. I hold back my questions, but she trails her fingers down the length of my arm, then clears her throat, preparing to say more.

"When the Unseelie Court invaded our kingdom, the Seelie and Unseelie tore through our woods in battle. We were dragged into their war, and in the chaos, our royal family has been decimated. Every blood heir has been assassinated, except for me. I was the halfling child, usually forgotten. Suddenly, I became next in line for the throne. In order to protect the royal line, my mother disguised me as a human child and sent me to the mortal world. I was only seven years old."

We met back then, on the elementary school playground. That little girl, playing in the puddle, had really been trapped and completely alone. No real family, nothing but memories of her faraway home. All these years, she's endured me moaning about my daily troubles, and I never knew how much she suffered on her own.

Her hair brushes across her cheek, and I tuck it behind her ear. She catches my hand in hers. Instead of softness, concern etches itself into her features.

"I received word from my mother at the New Year. I traveled partway to Hawaii with Tim and Tina, but I never really went there, although they remember it differently. A Court knight intercepted me. The war is over now. It's nearly time for me to go home. I thought everything had come to an end, but now these dark elves have appeared here. They must be Unseelie knights."

"You mean Wolf and Raven are here to hurt you?" Their malicious eyes flash in my mind. Panic rises in my throat. Wolf and Raven are the evilest fae I've ever encountered, and I shudder to think what they plan to do to Caris.

But Caris only shakes her head. "The war has ended, and a treaty has been signed. My presence here must have been mentioned at some point, so they were able to find and recognize me despite the camouflage provided by my pendant. Still, they wouldn't breach the treaty now. Assassinating me at this point would break their oaths."

"Then what's going on?"

"I'm protected, but you aren't." Caris rolls onto her back. "The Unseelie Court must have sent spies. If that's the case, then they have noticed my connection to you. I can't think of any other reason behind their sudden aggressiveness. One of them must have used a pendant like mine to impersonate me today and fed you fae food. The Unseelie Court is using you to get back at my family."

My heart beats wildly in my chest. It wasn't Caris at the tennis club. A faerie tricked me, using the same magic that Caris has been using all this time to fool me into seeing her as human. Unlike Caris, though, this faerie was determined to harm me. This faerie was a predator. Like Wolf. I thought I'd imagined the red flash in Caris's eyes at the tennis club, but that sinister color had been a warning. I swallow hard and try to push past the terror rising in my throat.

"But I'm just a high school girl that can't even play tennis anymore," I say.

Caris chuckles softly. "It's a pathetic move, really. They've lost the war, and now they're trying to pick at our hangnails."

Apparently, I'm a hangnail. Or maybe Caris didn't mean it like that, but I'm not about to ask, or else she might tell me straight up that I'm a pebble in her shoe. Still, she kissed me, so I try not to take it to heart. No one kisses a pebble in their shoe. Unless faeries kiss for meaningless fun.

Caris said her father was human, that her mother didn't find him worthy of living in the faerie Court. If her own faerie mother tossed her human father out like a sack of garbage, then a kiss from Caris might be nothing more than a passing amusement. I could be as important to Caris as my hookup with Brad meant to me.

As though reading my thoughts, Caris leaves a whisper of a kiss on my lips. Before I can return the kiss, she stands. I can barely believe that she's getting ready to go. But that's Caris: uncatchable.

Stuffing down any attempts to tell her to stay, I shoulder off her jacket. When I hand it to her, she pushes it back into my arms. "Keep it," she says. "I should go. I need to check on a few things before sunrise, but I'll come by tomorrow. You'll be safe tonight. Trust me."

With that, she leaves through the window, closing it behind her with an imperceptible click. The air falls still, threatening to suffocate me beneath the weight of Caris's confessions and my thousands of worries. Caris said to trust her, but I turn on all the lights in my room anyway, like a toddler afraid of the dark.

Now that she's gone, I can't help but feel like she was

never here. I could wake up tomorrow, meet with Caris later in the day, and discover that this whole night was a dream or a hallucination.

I hug Caris's jacket close, breathing in her woodsy scent. Even if she isn't going away to college, I can't keep her here with me. Without Caris, I have only a fistful of failures and a bad reputation to carry with me into an uncertain future. If Caris leaves, then the only path I have to take is to a desert of loneliness in Arizona. I'm sick of not belonging. Staring down my empty bedroom, I'm struck by how much I've learned today, and yet there is not a single person I can talk to about it. If I told anyone at school, I'd be a laughingstock. Even my own parents would feel nothing but shame. To all of them, when it comes to faeries, I'm just the girl who sees imaginary creatures. They would never stop to think that, maybe, the things I see are the truth. And that truth is locking me in a cage. Without Caris, I'll always be in that cage by myself.

Caris has an entire faerie kingdom waiting for her homecoming. I'm stuck in the same old cycle of losing at everything I try to accomplish, all thanks to the faeries. But Caris is a faerie. She understands me. She knows that the things I see are real. She's a part of the world that no one else sees. If I could join her, I would be diving headfirst into a world more dangerous than anything I've ever dared to imagine.

But if she gave the word, I'd go anywhere. Anywhere, except staying here.

CHAPTER TWELVE

Waiting for Caris is the worst. She promised to visit, but she never said when, and the clock runs slower the more I watch it.

I pass the morning lying in bed and replaying Caris's kiss in my mind. I don't want to think too much of it, but the details float to the surface. The shape of her lips skimming across mine, the heat of her fingertips slipping beneath the jacket she lent me. My cheeks burn embarrassingly hot in my empty room, so I kick off the covers and decide to do something more meaningful with my time.

Grabbing my cell phone off my nightstand, I swipe past notifications about whatever party everyone whiled away their Friday night at. Jasmine posted a selfie with her pink tennis racket, boasting about a tennis scholarship she's been awarded. I don't want to take it personally, but given yesterday's locker room fiasco, she's probably taking a stab at me through social media. I don't even know why we follow each other, and yet I still don't block her. I guess I'm a masochist.

Caris mentioned that Wolf was probably harassing me to get back at her family. I have enough problems without a rabid elf stirring up trouble in my life. Raven seems to have taken a liking to Jasmine, too, following her at school and at the Kit Park kickback last week. I swipe my thumb across my phone screen to the web browser and type in *Seelie and Unseelie Courts*.

A bunch of pages about the occult crop up. I settle on one at random and skim through vague information about good and bad faeries. Apparently, the Seelie are the good guys and the Unseelie are the villains. A passage reads, *Neither the Seelie nor the Unseelie favor human life. All goodness runs dry when mortal lives are involved.*

"Sucks to be human," I say aloud. Basically, no matter which faeries I encounter, I'm the dirt they scrape off their boots. Just like Caris's dad. Has Caris been humoring me because she's got nothing better to do during her exile? Our quick kiss good-bye last night flashes in my memory. Somehow, I've wound up blushing again.

Annoyed with myself, I throw my phone on my bed and grab a fresh pair of underwear, a tie-dye shirt, and some sweats from my dresser. The sun burns through clouds outside my window, so I trade the sweats for jean shorts before heading to the bathroom.

As I pad down the hall to the shower, Dad calls good-bye from the doorway. Mom's farewell fades behind the bathroom door. The hot water runs down my head, curling my straightened hair. As I shave, I wonder if faeries shave, too. The thought of Caris running a razor over her legs no longer makes sense, because the blades are made of iron, right? I've never had to think twice, but the human world has been one disaster avoided after another for her.

I'm caught between feeling bad for Caris and getting mad at myself for thinking about her again. Am I really supposed to wait around all day for her to show up? In the end, I'm complaining about thin air, since I'm grounded and can't go anywhere anyway.

Out of the shower, I blow dry my hair into a poofy mess, then flat iron it into a straight sheet that falls just above my shoulders. The smell of burnt hair fills the bathroom, and I carry it in my nose all the way to the kitchen.

"Good morning," Mom says, even though it's already past noon. She's got grilled cheese on the stove. "Want one?"

My stomach growls at the sight of the gooey sandwich. "Yeah, thanks." I fill a glass with apple juice, then add as an afterthought, "Want me to heat up some soup?"

"That sounds nice," Mom says with this sweet smile that makes me regret all the lunches I've spent ignoring her while grabbing a sandwich to go.

In a few minutes, we've got grilled cheese and tomato soup on the table. Our spoons clink, and each crunchy bite feels a little unbearable in the heavy silence. I don't want her to bring up tennis, so I take a preemptive strike at the conversation:

"How's Grandma?"

"The same. Aunt Erin messaged me this morning about the chemotherapy. Grandma's doctor thinks her heart can't take another round."

"What does that mean?"

Mom takes a drink of water. "It means Grandma needs a break from chemo."

"But doesn't she need the chemo to treat the cancer?" I ask, and then I feel bad for asking, because the look on Mom's face tells me she doesn't want to answer that question.

"We'll be moving there soon to help out Erin."

Grandma is going to die. That's what Mom doesn't say. My parents are moving to Arizona to be there for Grandma's last days.

"You don't need to be worrying about this," Mom tells me. "Now that you're no longer practicing with Lanie, you should focus on school and on finding a job if you want to stay here. You can apply to community college. If you have a plan, then what's going on with Grandma doesn't have to put a pause on your life."

"Maybe I should go with you guys. I could help with Grandma, too."

Mom shakes her head. "We can fly you out when the time comes. Grandma would want to hear good news that you're headed in the right direction. You know her. She doesn't like a fuss."

More reasons to get my life together.

"What do you have going on today?" Mom asks, abruptly changing the subject, so I take the hint.

"Nothing much. I'm grounded, remember?"

She nods. "Do you have any homework?"

"I've got a government project that's going to take me all weekend just to figure out how to write the first paragraph." I'm not exaggerating. Mrs. de la Cruz assigns ridiculous essays in her monthly review packets. I don't even mention the page of trig problems that I'm magically supposed to solve by Monday.

"Maybe you can invite Caris over to help you?"

"Not like I can call her." I don't mention that Caris is already planning to stop by. After all, a golden opportunity has presented itself. "Do you think I could go over to her place?"

Mom is skeptical, but her phone call with Aunt Erin seems to have eclipsed the fiasco at the tennis club yesterday. Both my parents think of Caris as a good influence. She's been on the honor roll every semester since the third grade. I can't help but suspect Caris of glamouring her name on that list. Then again, words like *dalliance* and *formidable* were rolling off her tongue like water last night, so maybe elves are just naturally smarter than us basic humans.

After a melodramatic sigh, Mom narrows her eyes at me. "You can go, but I want you home before eight o'clock. Not a minute later."

My heart leaps in my chest. I'm so relieved that I've been released from captivity that I hand-wash and put away our lunch dishes instead of just throwing them in the dishwasher. In my room, I zip up my knee-length boots before tossing my government textbook and laptop into my backpack. Caris's jacket is the final touch. I'm about to dash out the door when I catch a glimpse of my mom frowning at her phone on the living room couch.

"I'll be back before eight," I say.

She smiles, just a little. "Don't get into trouble, Ashly."

The March sun warms the backs of my legs as I trek down the street. An orchard full of unripe avocadoes and oranges comes into view. I jump over a low wooden fence and pass the trees. As bad luck would have it, the sprinklers kick on, so I run the rest of the way to the neighborhood on the other side. Thankfully, my hair didn't get wet. I don't want to show up at Caris's doorstep with frizzy hair.

I roll my eyes at myself. Since when do I care about looking flawless in front of Caris? Her dark eyes inch into the edges of my thoughts, and I shut that down before I end up red in the face again.

Caris's one-story home sits between a three-story renovation masterpiece and a beaten-up house with a For Sale sign in the yard. I haven't been here since Tim and Tina invited me to Caris's low-key seventeenth birthday last year, but I'm pretty sure that house was for sale back then, too. There's no car in Tim and Tina's driveway, but that doesn't tell me much since they have a garage. I follow the plain cement walkway to the porch and ring the bell.

Tina answers the door. Her graying hair is in a ponytail, and she's wearing paint-splashed overalls. I didn't know she painted. Then I remember that she's a kindergarten teacher, which is both cute and weird. Cute because she has the patience of someone that wipes five-year-olds' noses, and weird because she has a wood elf princess for a make-believe daughter.

"Hi there, Ashly!" She actually claps her hands as she greets me. Tina's dark eyes resemble Caris's, without the hint of mischief. Between streaks of gray hair, brown peeks through. I can see glimmers of Caris everywhere, yet these echoes are mere coincidence. Or fragments of faerie glamour.

"Hey," I say. "Is Caris here?"

She taps her chin in thought. "You know, she was here just a moment ago, but she must have slipped out. I was looking for her to help me with dusting, and she disappeared."

I nod, not sure what to say to that, and she opens the door wider. "Why don't you come in? I'm sure Caris will be back soon."

Not willing to go home defeated, I accept her invitation. The living room is decorated like a country townhome with rooster artwork on the walls and baskets of fake fruit on the coffee table. I sit down on the paisley-print couch and drop my backpack to the floor.

A moment later, Tina arrives with lemonade and Tim in tow. Tim takes a seat in an armchair. His tan skin is a shade or two darker, holding on to remnants of their sun-filled vacation in Hawaii. Caris's skin glows with that same undertone of gold that never changes with the seasons. I always thought that being biracial was something that Caris and I shared. Now, as my gaze flickers between her adoptive parents, I feel the weight of her secret more than ever. Caris may not be human, but she isn't fully fae either.

We both teeter on the rickety bridge between two in-groups. Neither wholly one thing, not quite the other. While I hope that Caris's mother felt a pang of sorrow when she forfeited her daughter to the mortal world, there is always the possibility that it was an easy sacrifice. For the Queen at least. Caris said she had no interest in meeting her human father, but her opinion of her mother seemed lukewarm at best. The faerie world may be her true home. She doesn't have to wear an enchanted pendant there or hide her magic. All the same, the fae might laugh behind the back of the half-mortal princess, even if she is their remaining heir. Perhaps her human lineage is the reason she is the only heir that remains in her Court.

Tina fills our glasses. The whole thing feels like a page out of a family magazine. Without the glamour, Caris could never fit into this excruciating normalcy. I sip at the lemonade, but its sweetness puts me on edge. Basically, I'm waiting for some nightmarish faerie to wreck the cookie-cutter peace.

"How have you been, Ashly?" Tim asks. His T-shirt reads, *Hawaiian Time.*

"Can't complain." The lie rolls off my tongue with ease. Tim is a harmless guy, but he's just like every other adult. He doesn't want the real answer to that question. "I came over to ask Caris for some help with my government paper."

"She'll probably be home in a bit. I saw her this morning, but when I went to ask her to do some yardwork, she'd already run off somewhere."

I sip my lemonade, halfway expecting Caris to reappear out of thin air.

Tim turns to Tina. "Honey, why don't you grab those little chocolate cakes. I'm sure Ashly would like one."

I just ate lunch, but I don't want to refuse their hospitality. Tina returns with a box of snack cakes wrapped in plastic. Back in the third grade, I spent the night at Caris's house to celebrate the end of the school year, and Tim and Tina served these same cakes. Caris had sniffed hers and then thrown it in the trash when her parents weren't looking. After lights out, she raided the fridge for grapes and white cheese. Even then, she hadn't seemed to like the cheese all that much, but we ate until my stomach hurt. When I rejected breakfast in the morning, Caris nudged me under the table with the slyest grin on her face. Even I thought it was funny.

"How is tennis?" Tina asks.

"Any college plans? How about a Division One school for tennis?" Tim adds.

They're so clueless about my life that it hurts, but I'm not about to unload my woes on a couple that has more problems than they even know. A pang of commiseration squeezes my chest. Soon, their only child will vanish from their lives.

The front door creaks on its hinges as the familiar sound of Caris's boots clunks on the hardwood floor. When she steps into the room, her eyes dance around the scene in front of her. Before I can worry that she's annoyed to see me, the corner of her mouth eases into her signature lopsided smile.

"Look who's here, Caris," Tina says. "Ashly hasn't come to visit in a long time."

"You're impatient," Caris says playfully in my direction.

I feel the heat return to my cheeks and hope that it doesn't show through my tan skin. Luckily, Caris sidles to the kitchen and returns with an apple and a plastic bear filled with organic honey. With an air of nonchalance, she sinks into the couch beside us.

"What have you been up to?" Tina asks.

"A little bit of this and that," Caris says.

Tina looks like she's about to ask for more information, but her expression suddenly glazes over as if a wave of drowsiness doused her thoughts. "Okay," she mumbles.

I cast a wary look toward Caris, but she only pours honey directly on her apple's green skin. She sinks her teeth in, like what just happened to Tina was nothing strange. Like she was the one who made Tina forget her questions. Like she just glamoured Tina in the blink of an eye.

Tim doesn't seem to notice. "Ashly said she has some economics homework to do."

"Government," I correct reflexively.

Caris stands. "Perfect. Thanks for keeping Ashly company while I was out."

She gestures me toward the hallway. Right before we step into her room, she shouts over her shoulder, "I finished the yardwork and dusting."

"When did you do that?" I ask.

Caris shuts the door. "It's all in the wrist," she says.

I guess there's pros and cons to having a faerie for a kid. I'm piecing together a joke about Caris being demoted from royalty to housework faerie when she gently slips her fingers into my hair. My breath stills in my lungs.

"You're full of surprises," she murmurs. "I didn't expect you to come looking for me, but you're not one to sit and take orders."

As she speaks, she guides me toward the bed. Despite her statement about me not sitting and taking orders, I take a seat without question. "What were you doing this morning?" I ask.

"That's neither here nor there. Let's just say we have our work cut out for us tonight. We're going to the tennis club."

Carson is the last place I want to go right now. "No thanks. I'll pass."

"The tennis club is the only lead we have," she says. "So, humor me. It's time to lure out Wolf."

CHAPTER THIRTEEN

Caris leaves me on the bed and starts rummaging through her dresser drawer. Shockingly, she unearths a knife from beneath her clothes.

"What's that?" I ask, trying to affect the casualness of someone encountering a random photo album or secret pack of cigarettes.

Caris turns the hilt over her palm. "Insurance," she says simply.

The glint in Caris's eyes foretells that we won't be simply chatting with Wolf. Luring him out isn't where this afternoon will end. She wants to stop him in his tracks. While I'm fed up with faerie mischief, the knife is less comforting and more terrifying. I've always known that faeries are dangerous, but watching Caris run her fingers down the knife's hilt confirms my worst fears.

"What are you going to use that for?"

She raises an eyebrow. "It's for you."

The only weapon I've wielded is a tennis racket. Sure, I've shoved a few classmates in the school restroom, the ones who dared to put me down for kissing a few girls at a handful of parties, and the idiots that made jokes about me missing school to pick cotton with my dad. But knives are different. Its menacingly sharp edge could actually hurt someone.

"You keep it," I say.

"Don't be ungrateful. The blade is made of iron. That's more effective than anything else a human could use against the fae."

"Then why do you have it?"

Caris sits beside me on the bed. "This isn't the only weapon I have."

A lifetime of avoiding assassination isn't anything like the stories about princesses that I read under the covers when I was a little kid. While I've been waking up to my phone alarm and packing school lunches in the kitchen, Caris has most likely been running scared. Even so, she calmly places the knife into my jacket pocket like she's passing me a note in the hallway.

I hand the knife right back to her, careful to keep the blade off her skin. "It's yours, so you keep it."

Her eyes light up in amusement. "Stop being cute. Wolf is nothing like me. Unseelie are the most unpredictable foe you could face. He'll use your hesitancy against you."

"That's why you're coming with me, right?"

"Is that why?"

If Caris answered me this way just two nights ago, I would have thought she was being carelessly coy or poking fun at me for personal entertainment. Now I see through the illusion. She's avoiding my question because she doesn't want to answer honestly. Realizing this doesn't make her well-crafted response any easier to decode, though.

So then why is she coming with me to take on Wolf? After all, she mentioned that the Unseelie Court that decimated her kingdom couldn't hurt her anymore, all thanks to a spellbinding treaty. That makes Wolf my dilemma. Yet here she is, knife in hand, preparing to patch up my problems. But faeries don't fix anything. They start the fires.

She hops off the bed, then urges me by the elbow. As we head out, we find Tim and Tina watching a basketball game. The roar of the crowd fills the room.

"Homework finished already?" Tina asks.

A slow-motion replay starts, and Tim glances our way. "Oh, you got your old soccer ball out?"

"We want to get a little air before settling down with the essay," Caris says. She keeps pushing me forward, clearly unenthusiastic about small talk with her faux family. They call out farewell, and we escape to the porch.

"You glamoured your knife as a soccer ball?" I say as we step into the street.

"Tim and Tina think my bow and arrow are a badminton racket and a birdie that I keep on my closet shelf."

"That's creative. What would you do if they asked you to play with them some day?"

"They'd believe I won."

I bite my lip. "Have you ever glamoured me like that?"

Caris laughs. "Ashly, you have the Sight. There is no glamour that you can't see through."

Relief washes over me, but it quickly shifts to anxiety when I remember what we're planning to do. Carson Tennis Club is at least two miles away, but there would be no convincing Caris to call a cab. We settle into a comfortable pace. Still, each turn we take through the orchards and down neighborhood roads sends a wave of jitters through me.

"What exactly is the plan?" I ask once we reach Kit Playground. A group of little kids giggle as they run circles around the same giant animal sculptures where I saw Raven not too long ago.

"We force Wolf's hand. Once he reveals himself, we take him down."

While the knife in her hand may look like a soccer ball to any passerby, I wish she would put it away. As though reading my thoughts, she tucks the blade into one of her pants' belt loops.

The plan is vague, but I resolve to trust Caris. I can't recall a single time that she's put me in harm's way. Whether

I understand her intentions or not, she's helping me out. Complaining doesn't seem like a viable option.

As we approach the entrance to Carson Tennis Club, it hits me: I'm banned from the court. Word has no doubt reached all the club managers. I'm a familiar enough face that they'll kick us out the moment we step inside.

When I share this news with Caris, she seems unfazed. "They'll let us in."

Once we enter the tennis club, the manager at the desk frowns in my direction. His name tag reads *Connor*. He started working here around the same time I started high school, and we've never been on good terms. Of course, I haven't ever tried to be polite, and now I'm pissed at myself for my bad attitude.

"Listen, Ashly," Connor starts to say. Then his eyes glaze over as his mouth hangs open in a peculiar stupor.

"She has something she needs to take care of," Caris says. "So let us pass, and keep quiet about it." She continues striding toward the locker room corridor without waiting for a response. I follow but can't help but glance over my shoulder at Connor's dazed expression.

"Have a nice day," he says chirpily.

Caris goes straight to the locker room. A mother and her preteen daughter are changing into tennis clothes, but they don't seem interested in us at all. Once they leave, the silence of the locker room presses in. I'm at a loss for what will come next.

"I'm going to go to the restroom," Caris says, surprising me. Sure, it was a long walk from her house to here, but a bathroom break feels a little unwise at a time like this.

"I'll come with you," I say.

Caris takes me by the shoulder. "No, you stay. I'll be back in a few minutes."

With that, she leaves me in the last place I want to be by

myself. I march around the room, wishing she would hurry up. She even took the knife with her, though I doubt I'd be able to use it. Still, I feel completely exposed. Caris's presence is a weapon in and of itself, and after what happened only yesterday, I would rather be working on my government essay than be in this room alone.

After a minute, I start to worry that someone I know will enter the locker room. I may be able to see through glamour, but I can't produce it. It would be just my luck if Jasmine showed up. Unable to shake off the paranoia, I crack open Jasmine's locker. It's empty. She must have taken her pink duffel home for a wash after it wound up in the shower.

The shuffle of footsteps advances toward me from behind. I take a deep breath, ready to tell Caris off for abandoning me for so long, but when I turn, I find a pair of red eyes inches from mine. A scream dies in my throat.

"You're mine," Wolf whispers. I stumble backward, and Jasmine's locker door slams shut as I smash my back against the handle. My head crashes against the metal, and the world goes black.

❖

During the summer between kindergarten and first grade, Grandma came to visit. Like any reasonable parents, Mom and Dad took advantage of having a live-in babysitter and often went out on dinner dates.

I never minded. While my parents always made me eat all my vegetables, Grandma gave me dessert before dinner. She played hide-and-seek with me and pretended it was hard to find me. We watched more than an hour of TV together at a time, and I loved cuddling against her on the couch. Her perfume smelled like cinnamon.

We were watching a seventies rerun when I felt Grandma

go tense. Her gaze shifted from the TV screen to a lamp in the corner of the room. The shadow cast by the lamp twisted like vines, crawling toward us steadily.

"Time for bed, Ashly," *she said in a tone she used for moments when I wasn't allowed to get a word in edgewise. Even so, she planted a kiss on my cheek and patted my back as I crawled off the couch.*

"Good night, Grandma." *I shut my door behind me, but like any curious child, I cracked it back open. I expected to hear nothing but the old-timey dialogue of the show we'd been watching. Instead, the familiar click of the TV shutting off carried down the hall.*

"Go away," *Grandma hissed.*

At first, I thought she was speaking to me. As I was about to shut my door again, she continued, "There's nothing for you here. Just old magic that has long since worn out."

"Magic never wears out," *a strange voice creaked.* "Your ancestors may have died. You may die. Your children may never See us, but the magic never dies."

Terrified but full of wonder, I pushed past my door and tiptoed down the hall. Grandma stood in the center of the room. There was no one else in sight. Just the tangled shadow on the carpet.

"What do you want from me?" *Grandma asked. While she spoke softly, every word wore the strongest sternness.*

"When you live forever, a short conversation is enough to pass the time."

With her head high, Grandma crossed the room to the overhead light switch. "I'm too old for these faerie games."

"But we'll never grow too old to play games with mortals."

The overhead light flicked on, and the shadow disappeared. Grandma walked to where the shadow once festered, stomping a few times for good measure. Then she gently picked up the TV remote. The chatter of commercials filled the eerie silence with normalcy.

I snuck back to my bed and squeezed my eyes shut. I dreamed of the faeries in the garden, and when morning came, Grandma made pancakes for the whole family. Sometimes, when I was by myself in the living room, I would turn out the lights, but the shadow never reappeared.

I chalked it all up to a dream. The faeries were always with me, whether I was awake or asleep. I never saw Grandma speak to a faerie again, and soon, I all but forgot there had ever been a talking shadow on my living room floor.

❖

For the second time in two days, I wake up on the shower floor. Only this time, my head hurts like hell, and Caris is standing a few feet away. Wolf paces the lockers like an animal.

"You can't harm me," Caris says. "That breaches the treaty."

"You can't harm me either," Wolf says. "But I can hurt *her*."

With an ear-splitting clank, Caris throws the knife down at my feet. I scramble off the tile and make a grab for it, even though I can't imagine stabbing anyone. Even an Unseelie elf.

"What am I supposed to do with this?" I shout at Caris.

"Use it!"

"How?"

Wolf laughs as he saunters toward Caris. She raises her fist, as though to strike, but her arm jolts back. Rage blazes in her widened eyes. Just like Wolf said, she can't lift a finger against him. While her glare is more vicious than any dagger, her hands slump helplessly to her sides.

With a gleeful sneer, Wolf turns his attention toward me. I've never felt more exposed in my life.

"You have to fight back!" Caris shouts.

In a breath, Wolf darts forward, but thanks to Caris's warning, I'm not caught off guard like last time. On pure instinct, I shove him hard. He must not have expected a challenge, because he loses his footing and plummets to the ground. Fury overwhelms his features. He presses his hands into the floor, ready to hoist himself up and attack once more.

Adrenaline courses through my veins. While a hand-to-hand assault from a faerie is nothing like a tennis match, I know better than to miss a chance to exploit an opponent's weakness. I charge toward Wolf, raising the knife straight for his throat. But I falter. I'm a tennis player, not a murderer.

Wolf shrieks. As his eyes roll back in his head, the skin of his throat flushes bright red, then cracks into scorched blackness. The iron blade is burning through his skin.

He claws at my hand, and I nearly drop the knife as I withdraw a few steps. The burn on his throat begins to crumble, flakes of singed skin floating in the air. He's coughing in pain, but his arm reaches out for me again, which douses any hopes that he'll surrender.

That means I can't back down either. This elf comes from the same Court that killed all of Caris's siblings. He's been playing cat and mouse with me, and it's my choice whether I become his prey.

Before he can stand again, I lash out. This time, I press the knife against his face. His cheek blackens into a charred monstrosity, and the acrid smell is worse than anything I've ever breathed in. His howls crush my ears.

In a flash, Caris strides to my right. "Make an oath that you will never come near Ashly or her friends or family again."

"I make the oath!" he moans.

I start to retract the knife, but Caris grabs my wrist to hold it in place. "What do you swear?" she insists.

"I swear that I will never touch this Ashly of yours or her familiars."

Caris releases my arm, and I drop the knife. Uncontrollable tremors take over my hands. The burns on Wolf's face and neck gape wider than any gash.

He spits onto the floor. "Curse both of you," Wolf says.

Caris mocks his empty threats. "Go back to your Court in shame."

As if ushered by her words, his body begins to fade like mist. "The treaty only lasts for a century. You and I will live far longer than that, and then I will find you, and your family line will die."

After his body completely vanishes, his voice echoes off the locker room walls: "You won't be so lucky with my sister."

CHAPTER FOURTEEN

Writing a government essay after a near-death experience with an Unseelie elf is bizarre, to say the least. Thankfully, Caris knows her way around a five-part essay, because we knock it out in a couple of hours. Every time I try to bring up the events of the day, she simply replies with some variation of "You did well." Her unwillingness to talk is just short of infuriating.

At least she walks me home. After we climb the steps of my front porch, I shoulder my backpack and prepare for an unnaturally normal good-bye, but she takes my hand, and my heart stills.

"What happened today is typical for the fae," she says. "Don't let it concern you."

"Got it."

She shakes her head. "So long as I'm near you, the Unseelie will see you as my weakness. The fae are dangerous, but our world is vast. There is just as much beauty as there is cruelty."

I remember the slumbering faeries in the garden, the light of the pixies in the woods, the sweetness of Caris's mouth on mine. In some small way, faeries are a lot like humans, even if they would scoff at the thought. We are all a mess of struggle and triumphs. Whether through gimmicks or glamour, we're faking our way to good times.

"You might have been better off without the Sight," Caris says.

"Could you make it go away?"

Caris unwinds our fingers, only to place her hand on the small of my back. "Would you want me to?"

Without the Sight, I could have tennis. My teachers would stop blaming me for the mishaps I thwarted against mischievous classroom faeries. My parents would stop worrying over every little thing. I wouldn't have to keep others at an arm's reach. I could have friends.

But if I lost the Sight, I would become like everyone else: helpless against a world they can never see. I would shrug off missing items as my own absentmindedness. I would blame the people around me for faerie tricks. All the while, the fae would laugh at me, but I would never hear it. I wouldn't be able to join in their laughter when they pulled harmless pranks, like trading Mrs. Carmel's coffee for water or switching the contents of my dad's underwear drawer with my mom's. The nights would be darker without their little lights. The woods and the garden would be empty.

Caris would be nothing more than a straight-A student who left for college one day to never be seen again. And then I would have to play the role of jilted best friend. I'd have to pretend like I'm waiting for her to come visit someday, and I'm exhausted by all the pretending. But the only way I could shed my façade is to join Caris's world. The fae aren't afraid of my Sight. To them, I'm a documented human phenomenon. To be myself, even in a completely different world, would be far better than putting on an act for the sake of friends or tennis or my parents' approval.

"I'm the girl who came straight up to you in the third grade, when no one else could see you messing around in puddles," I say. "I don't want to change that. I'd rather be the only one who knows the truth, even if I get in trouble for it."

Caris brushes her nose against mine. "You're tough enough for the fae."

Our lips meet, and I know for certain that I would never give up Caris. Some faeries may hurt humans, and Caris might be leaving for her court soon, but I would never trade her memory for blissful ignorance. I want to keep her in whatever way I can.

When we part, she is smiling. "I couldn't take away your Sight even if I tried."

"What was that all about, then? Were you testing me?"

She starts down the porch stairs. "Good night, Ashly. Sweet dreams."

Like a blessing, I sleep through the night and wake with a head full of happiness.

❖

Returning to school after a near-death experience with an Unseelie elf is painfully normal. The bells ring, a hot Santa Ana wind rips down the halls, and I'm penciling in a final attempt at my trigonometry homework before first period.

I turn in my trig homework. I pass my government essay forward while Mrs. de la Cruz writes the next unit's name on the Smartboard. My planner app is a mess of due dates I doubt I can meet. The one day I wish I could mark is when Caris plans to leave. She won't tell me. Then again, I haven't asked. If we avoid the conversation, then she won't have to be honest, and I won't have to count down the days.

Yet it still feels like I'm counting.

Three times. That's the number of kisses she's gifted me, and the fact that her kisses feel like presents means that I have no idea what we are doing. If this were anyone else, I'd be ten steps ahead, prepping for *the talk* and plotting to never see that person again. I've never kept a steady girlfriend or boyfriend.

There's no point to dating someone long-term when you're pretending that there aren't faeries watching us hook up. Until Caris.

Caris would kick the faeries out the door. Or the fae wouldn't dare to show up at all.

I've missed half the lesson, and I'm stuck with more homework on a topic that is as far from faeries as reality can get. What's worse is that I can't find Caris at lunchtime. This isn't uncommon. Most likely she's glamoured her way off campus, but I can't help but wonder if she's avoiding me, even if that doesn't make any logical sense.

I buy a Pop-Tart from the student store and eat under the bleachers, and when the school day finally ends, I resign myself to a lonely cab ride home. Except when my feet hit the curb, there's a tap on my shoulder. As luck would have it, it's Brad.

"Go away," I say. My patience is stretched pretty thin.

"C'mon, Ashly," he says. "Can't we just chat?"

"Sure, tell me all about your life. I'm all ears."

He crosses his arms. "I was gonna offer you a lift home, but now I'm second-guessing my charity."

"Cut the good guy act. A ride with you would cost me something."

"Only an arm or a leg. You choose."

While he's only bantering, I've spent too much time with knives recently to shrug off a violent joke. The crackle of the blade against the Wolf's skin is permanently etched into my memory.

"Just tell me what you want and save us both the pain," I say.

Brad runs a hand through his sandy blond hair. "I saw you leaving government today, and you seemed out of it. We both have Mrs. de la Cruz, so I thought you might want my notes."

"Your kindness is out of character."

"We've been at the same school since junior high, and I'm going out of state for college. Maybe we should just let the past be the past, you know?"

My phone pings. A notification announces that my Uber is arriving in three minutes.

"Look, Brad. That's a cute idea and all, but your girlfriend and I just had a showdown last Friday, and I don't think you should be seen with me right now."

His brow furrows. "She told me all about it. She said that you're disqualified from tennis. Are you okay?"

"Everyone thinks I trashed Jasmine's gear, and you're asking me how I'm doing?"

"That's just it. I don't think you did it."

I'm stunned into silence. In all these years of bearing the blame, I never expected Bradley Jameson to stick up for me. It's too ludicrous to be true. "I'm sure you told Jasmine just that."

"I did."

His words fall like a bowling ball onto the sidewalk. He grins sheepishly and scratches the back of his neck. As if the situation couldn't be more awkward, my Uber pulls up beside us. I could get inside, wave off Brad, and drive away from any new problems that are biting at my heels. But I remember what he told me at Kit Park the other week: *I felt like we were in the same boat.*

I knock on the window of the cab. "Can you wait five minutes?" I say.

The driver is more than a little annoyed, but I promise a hefty tip. He rolls the window back up without answering, but he keeps the car in the park, so I figure we've come to an agreement.

"You've got five minutes to explain yourself," I tell Brad.

"I don't know, Ashly. It doesn't sound like something you'd do. Jasmine said it's not the first time you messed with people's stuff in the locker room, but that makes it sound even less believable. You've got a temper, yeah, but you're not an idiot."

"How did Jasmine react?"

He cracks his knuckles. "She broke up with me."

"I'm sorry," I say before I even know what I'm apologizing for. A nagging sensation saws at my gut that feels a lot like shame. I've been called a boyfriend stealer before, but this is the first time someone presented hard evidence that I caused a breakup.

Brad sighs. "I guess that's why I wanted to talk to you. Could you tell me what happened, just so I know for sure? Did you really throw all her stuff in the shower?"

"No, I didn't."

"Then who did?"

No matter how understanding Brad is currently trying to be, faeries would be too much to swallow. "Probably the same person that knocked me out in the locker room."

"Why would someone do that to you?"

I roll my eyes, and Brad laughs, because we both know that there are lot of people at Hackley that would be happy to see me screwed over. Then his laugh fades into a frown. Whatever he's about to say, it isn't easy for him.

"Do you think Jasmine did it?"

While Jasmine and I are mortal enemies, I'm not about to take advantage of the situation and slander her name. "No, she wouldn't go that far."

"I don't know. She really hates you. She says you're crazy and that you're the worst part of her high school experience. I couldn't tell you the number of times I've had to listen to her rant about you." He clears his throat. "Maybe I shouldn't tell you that, though."

"Why not? Are you afraid she'll hear?"

He shakes his head. "Nah, that doesn't worry me. It's just

that most people don't like hearing what's being said about them behind their backs."

He's right. It's one thing to face Jasmine face-to-face and another to learn the depths of her hatred for me from another source.

"Are you coming or not?" the Uber driver shouts out the window.

"I gotta go," I say, surprising myself with my reluctance to leave.

Brad opens the car door, which kind of makes me cringe but also feels nice at the same time. "We're graduating soon," he says. "We're almost done with all this small-time bullshit. No one can actually stop you from playing tennis unless you let them. It's your life, not theirs."

He shuts the door, which is a good thing. I don't want him to see the tear that slides down my cheek.

When I get to my house, there's no one else home yet. I head straight for the garage. I grab some rope off Dad's tool board and five tennis balls from the storage shelf. Once back inside, I collect my tennis racket from the hallway closet, retrieve five plastic cups from the kitchen, and balance the load to the backyard.

After tying the rope between two trees, I line the cups a few feet from each other and cross to the other side of my makeshift net. The felt of the tennis ball brushes against my fingertips. I toss it into the air and swing my racket. In the blink of an eye, the ball knocks over the first of the cups. I reach for another ball and aim. The second cup falls. Then the third and the fourth and finally the fifth.

A whistle cuts through the air. I don't have to look over my shoulder to know that it's the flower pixies cheering me on. I smile but don't gloat for long. The cups need to be reset. I haven't even broken a sweat yet.

CHAPTER FIFTEEN

Two days until spring break and Hackley is split into those who skip, those who argue with teachers, and those who are already on vacation in their minds. While I'm tempted to join the ranks of the chronically absent, my diploma is on probation, so I suck it up and daydream in between attempting notes. Once third period ends, I drag my feet to the vending machine. Nothing but Gatorade and water. I wish Hackley was one of those prestigious schools that sell coffee and espresso. Instead, I'm feeding a couple of dollars into the machine, hoping that red Gatorade contains trace amounts of caffeine.

"I wouldn't drink that if I were you," says a voice that I haven't heard for three days now. I whip around and wrestle with whether to scold Caris for her disappearance or hug her harder than ever. She makes the decision for me. With her arms around my shoulders, I decide to forgive her for going AWOL.

"How are you going to keep up your grades with all these absences?" I tease once she releases me. While she has a penchant for vanishing from school, I couldn't help but worry that she wouldn't come back this time.

"Somehow, I think I'll manage."

The Gatorade clunks to the dispenser box. "Where have you been?"

"Over the river and through the woods. Apparently if you

take the right turn, you might find a messenger from a faerie court."

"What did this messenger want?"

Caris shrugs. "He briefed me on the goings-on in my family's Court. There may have been some details about my eventual return, or maybe he left me with more questions than answers. Either way, I told him about Wolf."

"Good. The Unseelie Court tried to break the treaty, right? That should get them in trouble."

"The treaty still stands. I'm unharmed, but it would've been irresponsible of me to keep my family in the dark about an attack like that."

I sip at the Gatorade, and Caris grimaces. Since passing period is nearing a close, we make our way toward the quad. From there, Caris and I will split for our separate classes. I slow my pace, trying to keep her for a little longer.

"Will you be around for spring break?" I ask. "Or is there more faerie business to take care of?"

"I'm all yours. I'll happily take you through more muddy forests and down dirty haunted pathways if you'd like."

I laugh. "You know how to get a girl's heart racing. Let's keep things calm for a bit. I'm not looking to get into another fight with Unseelie tyrants for a few weeks."

I expect Caris to needle me with more awful spring break plans, but her face stills. She peers beyond my shoulder. There's a part of me that readies to run. Oath or no oath, Wolf could be behind me, preparing to take revenge. Or worse, Raven might be flying in for a kill.

With a shaky breath, I turn around. No faeries in sight. But Jasmine is crossing the quad at lightning speed, straight for me. Sure, she's not a faerie with bared teeth, but she takes a solid second place for most obnoxious encounter.

"You pathetic bitch," she shouts over the few tables that separate us. Her curse is loud enough to catch the attention of the nearby students. By the time she reaches me, there's already a small crowd forming around us. The tennis princess versus the neighborhood bad girl. Line up and enjoy the show.

"What did you say to Brad?" she practically snarls.

I raise my eyebrows. Brad and Jasmine are well on their way to earning the graduation award for Most Dramatic Couple. While I could walk away and let her spit curses at me all the way to fourth period, I'm not about to let someone humiliate me in front of a crowd. If Jasmine wants a showdown, then she's chosen the right person to mess with.

"Last I checked," I say, "Brad walked up to me after school on Monday, and we had a little heart-to-heart that *he* initiated. So, why don't you ask Brad what he said to me. I don't have time to fix your relationship."

The red that tinges Jasmine's face is the purest color of rage. "Fix my relationship? You're the one who's taking out your tennis failures on me. What did you say to him, Ashly? He broke up with me because of you."

This is news to me. When Brad and I spoke on Monday, he seemed sincere enough. While he may be holding on to hope for a hookup, I seriously doubt that he was vying for a date on Monday. Jasmine is delusional or looking for someone to blame. I'm about to point this out when Caris grips my elbow. While I appreciate that she doesn't want me to risk suspension over a petty argument, I don't need to be held back yet.

But she yanks my arm sharp enough to jerk me backward. I follow her gaze, wondering if the principal has joined the crowd. I wish it was the principal, because Raven is sitting on top of a table only a few yards away. Her legs are crossed coquettishly, her chin resting in the palm of her hand. Those ice blue eyes pierce straight through me. The fire I was about to unleash on Jasmine freezes and shatters into a thousand shards.

"You're not even denying it," Jasmine says.

I blink in her direction. Our fight is suddenly so insignificant now that Raven is glaring daggers my way. "I thought you broke up with him last weekend," I manage to say.

"It was just a break. But when I went to smooth things over, he wasn't hearing it. He kept saying that I had it out to get you, that you aren't really that bad. What did you do, Ashly? What sob story did you sell him? Or is it that you're so desperate for a prom date that you had to go steal someone else's?"

A wave of *oohs* erupts from our audience. Her insult bounces off me, though, because Raven has chosen this moment to stand. The black feathers that make up the shoulders of her jacket tremble with each step she takes toward me. Caris's fingers dig deeper into my skin, which is my signal to go. But if I run away now, everyone at Hackley is going to stroll into spring break thinking that I stole Jasmine's boyfriend. I have enough enemies as it is, faeries included.

If I can get the last word in, then at least I'll have one less reason to hate my life.

"Look, Jasmine, I don't need Brad, and I don't need you blaming me for all your problems. No one here thinks you're as perfect as you believe you are. Trash collects trash. So just back off and mop up your own shit."

I might have gone too far because Jasmine throws off her bag. In a breath, she crosses into my personal space. Our noses are a mere inch apart. Just behind us, Raven draws closer. A sharp-toothed sneer hangs from her pale lips.

"You take and take," Jasmine shouts. "But we're all going to graduate, and you'll be stuck here with nothing and no one. Washed up, hung out to dry. I wish I could say that I'll be there to laugh at your worthless life, but I'll be gone, doing better things that you can only imagine. Go ahead and burn everyone around you. You'll be lying face-first in the ashes all by yourself."

The crowd breaks into applause at Jasmine's string of

insults, and I'm seeing red. Maybe she was once a friend, a harmless rival, but through the years, Jasmine has transformed into something monstrous. There could be a thousand reasons why she hates me, or a thousand reasons why she needs someone to squash to feel better about herself, but right now, all I know is that she's crossed the line. In the last week, I've burned a faerie's throat to smithereens. Jasmine is a wimp compared to Wolf.

I rip my arm out of Caris's hand and shove Jasmine with the same strength I'd pour into a forward swing. She tumbles backward as our audience gasps and roars. I'm about to feel good about the fear in her eyes, but the wind is knocked out of me as Raven breaks Jasmine's fall.

Raven's long fingers snake over Jasmine's shoulders. I nearly shout, "Watch out!" but I bite my tongue, even as I back up straight into Caris. Jasmine can't see the dark faerie. If anything, she seems relieved that she didn't plummet to the ground.

"What's going on here?" Mr. Spagnola comes rushing into the crowd and heads straight for me and Jasmine. The bell rings, and the students scatter in multiple directions. No one wants to get questioned about the fight.

Mr. Spagnola takes in the scene. Caris and me on one side, Jasmine on the other. He can't see Raven, but she sees everyone. Jasmine is still in her clutches, and the expression on Raven's bloodless face spells out victory. I have no idea what she's won.

"Get to class, ladies," Mr. Spagnola says. "Spring break is two days away. Don't make me write referrals now."

I don't need to be told twice. Caris heads toward the direction of my next class, and I follow with my head down. I hear Jasmine spouting excuses about a small disagreement to Mr. Spagnola. Caris and I turn the corner, but before we make our escape, I glance over the remnants of the war zone.

Raven is gone. It's even worse than if she'd stuck around.

❖

Jasmine doesn't do the morning announcements the next day. For the first time, I wish she had. I can't shake the image of Raven holding on to her like a bird of prey gripping a hissing kitten. Caris hasn't been any help either. Her strategy is to stay calm and avoid Jasmine. "You aren't equipped to take on another Unseelie," she warned. But if I don't stand a chance, what about Jasmine?

Homeroom ticks by. Spring break is a few hours away. I want nothing more than to bury my head under blankets for days. Everyone else can go on wild trips to the Bahamas or kickback in Kit Park each night. A week of solitude sounds perfect to me. Except Caris can come. She's the only one that saw Raven, the only one who understands what it's like to pretend not to see.

When homeroom ends, I take refuge in the restroom again. My reflection is haggard. Dark circles ring my eyes, and my hair could use another pass through the straightening iron. The wrinkles in my uniform speak miles about my state of mind. If I can make it to class, I can make it to Caris.

I splash cold water on my face as a girl exits a stall. She looks like a freshman. Her face carries baby fat, and her eyes linger on me warily. She could have been in yesterday's crowd, or she might have heard a rumor or two. Ashly Harris: the girl who shoved pretty Jasmine Bennett in the quad after stealing her boyfriend. Brad hasn't shown his face, which could mean he's skipping or that he took some extra days off before the break. I don't want to see him anyway.

"Are you okay?" the freshman asks.

"Yeah, it's just a bad day."

She rifles through her backpack. "Want some gum?"

After getting drugged by faerie chocolate, I don't take candy from strangers anymore. "I'm good, but thanks anyway."

"That was pretty cool," she says. "The fight yesterday. That girl seemed out to get you. Did you really steal her boyfriend?"

"No. I don't need to steal people's boyfriends."

She pops her gum. "Well, good luck. Hopefully everyone will forget by the end of spring break."

I nod, and she walks out the restroom. It's true. High school moves faster than a bullet. By the end of spring break, another couple will have broken up or a classmate will drop out or someone might wind up in the hospital. My social status has never been high enough for me to crash to the bottom. I can wait this one out for a week. Caris and I can relax, surf the net, buy organic snacks, and maybe sneak in a kiss or two. Or three. I squeeze her jacket against my chest. The freedom bell will toll at 2:40 p.m.

The restroom door swings open again. Since I'm not looking for any more small talk, I smooth down my hair one last time and head toward the exit. But that would be too easy. Today was never going to be easy.

Jasmine Bennett stands in the doorway, her hands on her hips and her red mouth crooked into a leer. I've seen her glare from multiple points of view, but this one takes the cake. She looks like a predator. It's almost enough to give me chills, but this confrontation is different from the quad. There's no crowd. No need to save face or spew out insults. One-on-one, I can take Jasmine down before she could land a slap.

"Move," I say.

"You move, mortal," she replies. Her voice is cold, frigid shards of ice pointed straight for my head.

The word *mortal* has never entered Jasmine's vocabulary. She's called me a homewrecker, deadweight, pathetic disgrace, the list goes on. But mortal is new. Mortal is distinctly fae.

"Excuse me?" I say.

"You foolish humans think you can hurt an Unseelie and never reap the consequences. You've disgraced my brother, and now I will destroy you. This girl hates you so much, she makes the perfect host. So long as I live inside her, you cannot burn me with iron. If you do, you might kill her, too."

As much as I hate Jasmine, I could never kill her.

Jasmine's hands reach for me, but they aren't her hands anymore. Raven said she lives inside her. She is controlling Jasmine's body, her mouth, and her mind. My blood freezes in my veins. Raven has me cornered. A shove won't stop Jasmine this time. The spite in her eyes is magnified, intensified by Raven's infinite hatred.

"That weak princess is nowhere to be seen now," she says. "She can't protect you, but if you bow and beg for mercy, I may leave enough of you to bury."

I'm not about to wait to die. I throw my entire weight toward the door, knocking past Raven and diving straight into the hall. Her nails tear at my sleeve, but the force of my mad dash is enough to rip my jacket from her grasp. I fall on all fours onto the cement. My knees burn, the skin tearing. But now isn't the time for pain. I jump to my feet and race to class, like I'm scared I'll be late. But really, I'm running for my life.

CHAPTER SIXTEEN

Racket in hand, I'm pacing the garden at midnight. I have nowhere else to go and no idea how to move forward. Instead, as always, I'm biding my time. Waiting for Caris to come over. Waiting for Raven to show up. Waiting for the faeries to come to me, because I'm powerless to make them do anything or stop them from doing anything.

The pixies in the hellebores aren't even paying me any attention. The urge to pummel all the flowers with my racket tenses through my arms. But hurting a handful of harmless fae in the name of stress relief is a low blow. I settle for collapsing on the grass. The stars in the sky won't even make an appearance on this cloudy night.

After several minutes, I decide I'm done waiting. After I escaped Raven in the bathroom, I'd barely kept my panic at bay in class until the bell rang. When I finally met Caris in the hall, I pulled her aside and told her every detail of Raven's attack. Her face darkened as she spoke a single word, *Possession.* A shiver had passed down my spine. I've dealt with faerie pranks my entire life, but Wolf and Raven are out of my league. Instead of allaying my fears, Caris simply turned away. As she headed down the hall, she called over her shoulder, *We can't talk here. I'll find you tonight.* The crowd of students milled around her until I could no longer see her among the swarming bodies. There were too many people. Too many ways that a faerie could hide in the horde. And I was alone, suddenly more aware of my mortality than I'd ever been before.

I need answers from Caris, and the only way to get real answers is to directly ask for what I want. It's a long walk to Caris's house, but anything is better than sitting around like a princess in a tower.

There aren't enough sidewalks in my neighborhood for me to feel safe walking the streets at night. Hopefully, my white hoodie and sneakers will alert any cars of my presence. The last thing I need is to wind up on the news as the first casualty of spring break. My parents would purchase my ticket to Arizona before I checked out of the hospital.

The avocado and orange orchard is a welcome shortcut during the day, but by night, the shadowy aisles of trees look more like a Halloween maze than a carefree stroll. By the light of my flashlight, I trudge through the damp dirt. The wind rustles through the leaves, and a twig snaps in the distance. I shake off my jitters. There's nothing out here but squirrels and stray cats. But if Raven were here, I'd never see her in the darkness.

Get a grip. I tighten my hold on my phone and double-check that I still have service. I'm about halfway through the orchard when another twig snaps. I huddle against the trunk of an orange tree. My flashlight picks up nothing but shadows.

"Don't mess with me," I shout into the night, just in case something or someone is out there. Thankfully, my voice doesn't shake.

"Is that a challenge?" someone says from behind me.

I whip around the trunk and cast my flashlight on the figure. My fear thaws. It's only Caris, squinting at me in the light.

"Thank God it's you," I say.

"Who else were you expecting?"

While her sassiness is typical, I could use a hug more than banter. I'm not about to tell her that.

"I wasn't expecting anyone," I say.

She leans against the tree trunk, hands in her jeans pockets. A lock of dark hair cuts into her eyes. "Then who were you talking to?"

I shrug. "You never know."

"I was going to see you, but I'm guessing you got impatient again."

"Well, what took you so long that you're just now showing up only halfway to my house? It's almost one a.m. Raven could have broken into my place and dragged me to the Unseelie Court by now."

It was meant to be a joke, but the grim possibility hangs heavily in the air. There must have been a hint of hysteria in my voice because Caris reaches for my hand. I'm embarrassed that my fingers are trembling. Thankfully, she doesn't mention it. She merely smooths her fingertips across my skin. The tension flows out of my shoulders and melts away, if only a little.

"All we know is that Raven has possessed Jasmine," Caris says. "Whatever she's planning most likely doesn't involve breaking into your house. She could do that without Jasmine. She's got something more nefarious on her mind. Something calculated. Vengeful."

"You know, when humans piss each other off, we just trash them on social media."

Caris shakes her head. "And you start wars. You build weapons out of iron and kill. You light forests on fire with the hope of burning your enemies to death. You even spread diseases to destroy each other. I took the same history classes as you."

"Maybe I wasn't paying attention."

She's right, though. Humans have been warring with each

other since before we knew how to write the stories down. Faeries are only more frightening to me because I have no idea how to fight them. Iron is the only trump card I've got. And Caris, but she doesn't even have a cell phone, so she's not a very reliable trump card.

"But really, where have you been? I mean, where were you tonight while I was waiting for you?" I make a point to be as specific as possible. She can't worm her way out of this question.

"I was off doing fae things."

"Which fae things were you doing tonight?"

She shakes her head. "Let's get out of the orchard."

"But you didn't answer my question," I say and shine my flashlight like a spotlight on her face.

She heads off without another word. My frustration is about a millisecond away from boiling over. Then again, Caris pulled this same trick back in the woods when I realized her faerie origins, so maybe this is about her family. Whenever it comes to her home life, Caris only spills the details behind closed doors. Almost every member of her family has been assassinated. I can't fault her for wanting privacy.

Tramping around in the dark is a lot less frightening with Caris by my side. She doesn't need a flashlight, but I still point my phone in the general direction of where we're going. We pass the street that would take us to her house, which means I have absolutely no idea where she's leading me.

To my surprise, we wind up at Callie's Diner. It's open twenty-four hours a day, and light spills from the windows. As we sidle up to the door, I can't shake the oddness of how ordinary it is to go to a greasy diner with a friend on a Friday night.

"So, this is more private than the orchard?" I ask. "I thought we'd go to your place."

She shrugs. "I try not to go there too much anymore. It's better that way. We all have to get used to what's coming."

While she doesn't say it outright, she must be separating herself from Tim and Tina. She's getting ready to go home. Her true home.

"Besides," Caris adds, as she pulls open the door with a hand covered by her sleeve, "a diner is better than the orchard. We can see who's around us. There's no telling who might be listening in on a conversation in the middle of nowhere."

Callie's Diner smells like pancakes and hasn't been renovated since its grand opening in the sixties. A single waiter loiters by the kitchen window. He's chatting away with whoever is cooking up the cheap eats.

"Look around," Caris says. "What do you see?"

A few patrons sit at tables and booths, chowing down on plates piled high with burgers, fries, and omelets. "There aren't any faeries."

"Exactly."

"But what if they're wearing a necklace like yours? They could be hiding in plain sight."

"A necklace like mine is rare, created by the ancient elf Mythias, and usually only worn by royals."

I don't point out that Wolf managed to get his claws on a similar design. Mythias might've struck a deal with more than one Court.

"The common fae wouldn't be able to afford one of his pendants," she continues. "It cost the Queen several heirlooms to convince him to forge it. I suspect it cost something more, but the Queen never shared the details. She only told me to be grateful. And not to screw things up."

Yet another responsibility for Caris to bear. Years of my parents' money wasted on tennis lessons can't compare to her family's expectations. The space between us is thick with our differences. Thankfully, the waiter notices us and heads in our direction.

"I should probably tell you that I didn't bring any money with me," I say.

"I have us covered." There's no outline of a wallet in Caris's back pocket, and she's opted for a black long-sleeve shirt instead of a jacket.

"Are you going to glamour some napkins into dollar bills?"

"What would you do if I did?" she says coyly.

"It's either that or dine and ditch."

The waiter's name tag reads Rob. As he guides us to a table, Caris smiles and pulls a twenty-dollar bill from her pocket. "My weekly allowance," she says.

It's ironic that Tim and Tina give her an allowance when she can literally make her own money. What's funnier is that Caris actually spends her allowance. I think there's a part of her that likes playing the role of mortal daughter. Her real parents are who knows how far away, and the only gifts they sent her off with are a knife, a bow and arrow, and a necklace.

"You must miss them," I say.

"Who?"

"Your parents, or at least your mom. The Queen."

"I hardly know my mother and I don't know my father at all. What's to miss?"

Caris flips open the menu, carefully avoiding its metal tips. I adjust my legs under the table so that she won't touch the table legs. Then again, Caris is wearing pants. I doubt that the iron content in the table legs is strong enough to burn her through her clothes. She's lived around iron for a decade. She knows the mortal world like the back of her hand.

"You could stay here," I say. "Instead of going back to the faerie Court."

Caris looks a little surprised and amused. "And who would I stay with?"

"We could be roommates. I'll get a job somewhere, doing *something*, even if it's just retail. You could glamour your way into any career."

She laughs. "I wouldn't waste glamour on a human career."

While a human career is child's play for her, I can't even fathom how to reach one. The big things for me are just laughing matters to a faerie.

"I would use my glamour to forge money and documents," she continues. "With that, I could open any business I want. Even if no one comes to the business, I could keep it running on glamoured funds. And I wouldn't have to worry about customers. There's plenty of common fae."

"You've mentioned the common fae before, but I'm gonna be honest. I have no idea what a common fae is."

"Faeries that don't belong to any Court. Some of them are exiles. Others were born and raised in exile centuries ago. They roam unclaimed lands, which means that they hang around mortals. Your tennis club is one of their gambling dens. At least underground. The common fae have tunnels running beneath Kit Park."

"That's only a little terrifying."

Caris calls the waiter over. "Can I have two orders of the vegetable plate, no butter, no seasoning. What do you want, Ashly?"

It shocks me how she can be so calm about underground gambling dens. "I'll have scrambled eggs and toast with sausage," I say.

Before the waiter leaves, she asks him to bring plastic silverware. In the past, I always thought of this as one of her quirks. Now I know better.

When the food arrives, I wonder if Caris's twenty-dollar bill is enough to cover both our meals, then decide not to worry about it.

Caris starts cutting her steaming vegetables into tiny pieces. "Would you rather have the common fae camping out beneath the tennis club or the Unseelie Court?" she asks.

"Neither. What about the Seelie Court?"

She snorts. "Just as bad."

"I thought your Court was fighting alongside the Seelie Court."

"For now. My family is what some might call a minor Court. There are dozens of minor Courts bordering the Seelie and Unseelie lands. We're known as the Court of Farrow Wood, and our kingdom lies directly between the Seelie and Unseelie. That's how we got caught in their war in the first place. It just so happens that the Seelie find it more advantageous for us to keep our Court. Better that than to have the Unseelie expand their territory closer to Seelie lands."

"So then, I'd rather have the Court of Farrow Wood burrow tunnels under Kit Park."

A slow smile spreads across her face. "We'd rather stay aboveground, in our woods, and mind our own business. Of course, if a mortal happens to stumble into those woods, that becomes our business."

"Or if the Unseelie stumble into your woods."

She nods solemnly. I haven't taken a single bite of my food, and my stomach growls over the smell of sausage, but the downcast look in Caris's eyes keeps me from digging in.

"I haven't forgotten," she says. "You asked me where I was earlier tonight. Where do you think I went?"

I have no idea. That's why I asked in the first place. Still, this is some sort of riddle. It's something about Caris that I can maybe untangle.

"You went home," is my first guess. Judging by Caris's raised eyebrow and laughing eyes, I'm dead wrong.

I suck in a breath and try to guess again. If Caris believes I can solve this puzzle, then there's a clue in what she's said to me tonight. She hasn't seen her faerie parents. She just told me that she's avoiding Tim and Tina's house. While I know where she hasn't gone, I'm unsure of where she could go.

Poring over our conversation, the answer strikes me. "You went to see the common fae."

It's so obvious that it makes me wonder how much of herself Caris has been sharing with me since we were kids. Signs that I never picked up. Hints she was waiting for me to piece together. *About time you figured it out.*

After all these years of her hoping I'd crack the code, I got mad at her for making me wait a few hours tonight.

"That's right," she says. "The common fae aren't the fondest of Court fae, but most of them were exiled at some point from the Seelie or Unseelie. The enemy of their enemy is their friend. I received word from the Queen that I should leave here on good terms with the common fae. In case of another war."

"Your family is already planning the next war? The treaty the Courts signed is that flimsy?"

What I've said amuses Caris enough to reawaken her appetite. She forks a crown of broccoli into her mouth. "The next war most likely won't be for another hundred years."

Faeries are immortal. Still, that's a long game plan to send Caris into the common fae's tunnels just to secure an ally for a war that may be a century away.

"If you went to see the common fae, doesn't that mean you revealed your true identity to them? I thought you couldn't tell anyone that you're a faerie."

"Eat, Ashly," she says. "I'm paying, after all."

I roll my eyes. After a few bites of lukewarm eggs and oily sausage, I gesture for Caris to continue.

"The Queen sent me a message, temporarily releasing me from my oath for the sake of meeting with the common fae, so I met with the common fae without my pendant. I wish she hadn't given me the order. Those tunnels are filthy, full of all kinds of human trash that those faeries collect like treasure."

"I want to see it," I say.

"Didn't you say the tunnels were terrifying just a minute ago?"

"It sounds kind of cool, though. Besides, it's not scary if you're with me."

"No," she says firmly and shuts her eyes. My stomach clenches around the greasy food I just ate. Caris takes a deep breath, then skims her fingers up my hand to my wrist until they rest heavily on my arm. When her dark eyes open once more, I couldn't move if I tried.

"Raven is enough to deal with," she finally says. "I'm not involving you further. For your own good."

Sure, if the common fae decide to target me, too, I'd be in over my head. Hearing her say it so plainly doesn't feel good, though. Despite her hand on my arm, she could be miles away.

"I'm already involved," I say. "You can't un-involve me. Besides, I spend just as much time with the common fae as you. If the common fae have tunnels or whatever under Kit Park, then I've been dealing with common fae all my life. Since there's a den under the tennis club, then all the faeries already know that I'm wrapped up with Wolf. That means they've figured out I'm knee-deep in Unseelie trouble. The damage was done the moment I was born with the Sight. So, you can't say it's for my own good—"

"How are you two doing?" the waiter cuts in. He freezes when he notices Caris's hand on my arm and clocks in the startled looks on our faces. Honestly, I feel a little bad for him.

"We're still working on our food," Caris says.

"If you wind up wanting dessert, we have green pie for St. Patrick's Day."

Pie spiked with green dye is the last thing Caris would ever eat. But she just nods, and the waiter walks to the next table.

"You're right," Caris admits for probably the first time in all the years we've known each other. "A mortal with the

Sight will always live beside the fae, but you don't have to live among us. We'll stop Raven. I'll return to my family. You can move forward from there."

Moving forward means following my parents to Arizona. It means never seeing Caris again. It means always being the crazy one.

"What if that's what I don't want?"

"You don't want to stop Raven?"

I sigh. "Of course I want to stop Raven, but what if I don't want to move on? Maybe I don't like being left behind."

Once I've said it out loud, I can't backtrack. Caris has to either push me off her train or buckle me in for the rest of the ride.

Her gaze shifts to the window, out to the dark street full of nothing but faeries scrambling in the shadows.

"One thing at a time," she says. Her answer is neither a yes nor a no. The uncertainty chokes me, but the lack of a solid no also sparks up a weak glimmer of hope.

"Let's figure out what to do with Raven," she says. "Once she's out of the picture, we can talk about next steps."

"Fine. Easy enough."

She lets go of my arm and bites into a forkful of soggy carrots. I take a stab at my toast. Suddenly, we're just two high school students, up way too late on the weekend.

"We can burn her, like we did to Wolf," Caris says, which effectively knocks me back into reality.

Raven's warning echoes in my mind. *If you burn me with iron, you'll kill her, too.*

"That's not really an option," I tell Caris.

"If it were me, I wouldn't care if Jasmine dies as collateral. Think about it. She's tortured you for years over a petty tennis rivalry."

"Pettiness isn't worthy of the death penalty."

Caris twirls her plastic knife between her fingers. "Mortal

ethics never cease to astound me. If you insist on doing things the hard way, there is another option. But it involves getting dirty."

"As in dirty work? I'm not committing any crimes this week. My diploma is on probation."

"You were willing to dine and ditch."

I point at her with my fork. "I had faith that you'd do the right thing."

"I'll do my best to live up to your expectations. And the dirty work only involves real dirt. As in mud, twigs, leaves. If we're lucky, we might get caught in a few cobwebs. We'll be completely crime free for now."

"Thanks for that," I say sarcastically. "When do we get started?"

"We'll start tomorrow at noon. I'll meet you at your place, and yes, I will show up on time. But I didn't come here just to talk. I haven't eaten all day. So, finish the meal I've so charitably bought you."

"You want to share the St. Patrick's Day pie?"

She throws a napkin straight at my face. "I'm feeling so generous that I'll let you eat the whole pie by yourself."

CHAPTER SEVENTEEN

The gnomes are back, *hup-hupping* on the porch swing, while I sit on the stairs with my head in my hands. Faeries get away with trespassing since no one can see them. Their racket may give me a headache, but I've got no one to complain to.

Thankfully, Caris comes into view down the street. I wave and hop off the porch, thankful that she's shown up like she promised. Stray gravel crunches beneath my Doc Martens. The Santa Ana winds died down last night, so I had to settle for jeans and a hoodie to combat the cool breeze. For good measure, I tossed on Caris's jean jacket. I'd rather her jacket take the brunt of whatever natural disaster she's planned for us.

"Ready for an adventure?" Caris says.

More like ready to hate the next few hours of my life.

"What torture device have you prepared?" I ask.

She continues down the street in the direction of Kit Park. "If you want to take Raven out without taking down Jasmine, there's going to be a sacrifice."

I stop in my tracks, boots skidding. "Caris, I'm not killing anyone or anything."

"Even an animal? What about a toad?"

"What the hell are you plotting?"

She laughs and grabs me by the jacket. Standing this close, her lips slightly parted, you'd think she was about to kiss me or murmur seductive words. Instead, she says, "What about a spider? Would you kill a fly?"

"You're kidding me, right? A fly is all it's gonna take to stop dark elf possession?"

She manages to step even closer. The heat of her chest radiates against me. I hope she can't feel my heart racing, and I'm more than a little annoyed that she's pulling these moves while talking about murdering insects. The fae are bizarre. Somehow, that weirdness is simultaneously alluring.

"Ashly," she says in my ear, "you're so gullible."

After a quick kiss on my cheek, she backs up. My face is burning, as she laughs at the cloudy sky. I cross my arms over my chest and mutter, "At least I can lie."

"Touché."

She continues walking, and I follow close behind. My jaw may be clenched with annoyance, but I can't help but bring my fingers to my cheek. The touch of her lips still lingers. I remember our fourth-grade field trip to the botanical garden. Caris hadn't talked much, her expression sullen and eyes glued to the countless flowers. I realize now, she may have been missing the Court of Farrow Wood. I ignored the sign that read *Do Not Touch* and picked a green stem lined with tiny blue flowers. When the teacher wasn't looking, I handed the flower to Caris.

"A bluebell," she said. She peered at me with her dark eyes, smiled softly, and kissed me on the cheek. Then she hit me on the nose with the flower. Pretending to be mad, I chased her until the teacher shouted at me to stop.

Even if Caris is messing with me, her games feel good. If only I could find a way to keep her in one place for longer than a moment. If only she'd stay put, then we could stop playing around. I could find out for sure if she's serious at all.

We reach the outskirts of Kit Park, but instead of taking the sidewalk, Caris heads straight for the woods. Even though the trees block out the wind, the temperature feels several degrees colder in the shade. Sure, it's warmer than Northern California or Washington, but I'm born and bred in San Diego. I haven't even gotten muddy, and I'm already daydreaming about a warm shower.

"Are we meeting with the common fae?" I ask. She still hasn't given me any clues on what we're doing.

"Ah, yes, the sacrifice. Well, perhaps I was being a little dramatic. You're cute when you're flustered."

"Stop with the teasing. There's a life on the line."

She picks a mossy branch off the ground and inspects it closely. "For today, all you'll need to sacrifice is keeping your clothes clean. We need to collect several ingredients for a stew of sorts."

"Vegetable stew is gonna fix Jasmine right up," I say sarcastically. "Why didn't I think of that? I've heard chicken noodle soup might be more effective."

"Not quite. There's a potion called the Purge. Only woodland elves know how to concoct it. If we make this potion and give it to Jasmine, then that should exorcise Raven's spirit from her body."

I'm impressed. Fae magic is so much more than whatever a Google search can dredge up. Somehow, Caris has managed to ace every subject in school and study the magic of her family's Court. Where she's found the time to hang out in my room is beyond my imagination.

"That could work," I say. "But how are we going to get Jasmine to drink the potion while Raven's in full control?"

"That's a bit more complicated. Raven doesn't have to drink the potion for the exorcism to take effect." She pauses in front of a bird's nest that I didn't even notice until she pulled the low branch to her face. "Thankfully, the Purge works so long as it hits a target's bloodstream. If we lace a weapon with the potion and manage to cut Jasmine's body, she'll be all better in a matter of minutes. Then Raven will have to retreat in order to recover from the Purge's less healing properties."

Caris crouches in front of a tree. Her fingers trace the lines of its bark and fiddle with a crop of nasty-looking fungus. After another second of investigation, she tears off that section of the bark and drops it in the drawstring knapsack she's been wearing.

"*Flavoparmelia*," she says. "That's one item on the list. Keep an eye out for red-capped mushrooms and let me know if you see any bird feathers."

We continue our trek through the forest. Birds chirp in the trees, and rabbits and squirrels rustle in the bushes. Caris kicks over fallen logs and trudges through mud puddles like a kid on a field trip. Everything looks green and yellow to me. There are no red mushrooms or bird feathers in sight.

As I uselessly search, a thought occurs to me. "Will the potion hurt Jasmine, too?"

Caris's eyes meet mine. "Why do you want to save someone who has done so many awful things to you?"

An eye for an eye. This could be the perfect opportunity to enact the worst of revenge. But I know firsthand how frightening the fae can be. I remember Wolf's cruel eyes screaming murderous rage. There's a difference between Jasmine's never-ending tirade against me and the desire to destroy someone. I've played the bad girl because of the faeries' mischief and madness. I won't turn into one of them. I won't become the villain that everyone imagines me to be.

"Jasmine is just a girl," I say. "She's mean and a little selfish, but at the same time, people like that—people like her are caught in a trap. When you're good at something, like getting straight As, or having a good boyfriend, or being a tennis star, then everyone starts to expect that from you all the time. I used to be the best at tennis. There were high expectations for me. I was supposed to be perfect. When you mess up, you get punished. Jasmine hated me because I always got in the way of her meeting everyone's expectations."

Caris plucks a feather out of another nest, but I can tell she's listening. Even as she places the feather in her knapsack, even as her eyes survey the ground, her whole body faces me. "Expectations are limiting," she says softly.

"In a way, the faeries saved me from that trap. I can never be what my parents or teachers or Lanie want me to be. I'm free to fuck up. Even if I can't help Jasmine in the end, no one will be surprised or disappointed. No one would even know. I don't have to save the world, but because of that, I can actually make a difference without being too scared to make a move. I'm the only one who can do this."

"And we will," Caris says. "You're different from other mortals, Ashly. You have more power than you can imagine, just by being human."

A bird takes flight above us and sends a flurry of dry leaves into the air. When Caris slides her hand along my waist, I can feel that bird's wings fluttering in my chest. Her lips meet mine, and I kiss her like she might disappear when we part. She's going away soon, leaving the human world behind. Leaving me behind. Every part of her will be unreachable. This moment may be nothing but a fleeting dream, but I can kiss her now. I can lose myself in her until I lose her forever.

When she pulls away, I expect a teasing glance or word. But she places her forehead against mine, and I hold her in this way for as long as possible.

"We'll save her," Caris says, and the spell is broken. "Since Jasmine isn't fae, the potion won't harm her. No one will die."

"Thank you."

Finding the remaining ingredients proves to be a grueling task. Caris has us crawling through bushes and digging into the mud for clay. My nails are caked with dirt. Twigs cling to my hair. When I point out a red-capped mushroom beneath a tree root, Caris pulls me into a hug. Her laughing smile and sharp eyes remind me of the girl I found playing in rain puddles all those years ago. We might not be screaming in slides anymore, but we're still the wild pair from back then.

Caris sticks her hand inside a hole in the ground, which basically defies everything I've ever learned about basic nature safety measures. After she pulls out a tuft of brown fur and sticks it in her bag, she announces, "We have everything we need."

"That's the best thing I've heard all day."

There are streaks of dirt on my hands, and my boots are caked with mud. Caris looks the same as when we started. I guess elves from the Court of Farrow Wood know their way around the forest.

The sun is halfway past the horizon when we emerge from the woods. By the time we make it to my home, the sky is completely obscured by dense clouds. A mist envelops us, wet and cold. The gnomes are nowhere in sight.

"You want to come in?" I ask Caris.

"Tempting, but there are a few more things I need to prepare for the Purge. Will your parents be home tomorrow? We need to use the kitchen."

"They usually go out for dinner on Sunday nights. It's their date night."

Caris hands me her knapsack. "Hold on to this."

It's time to say our good-byes, yet Caris seems hesitant to step away. She watches me closely as I shoulder her bag. The intensity of her gaze unnerves me. Her thoughts are locked away. The memory of her kiss stings my lips. I'm always waiting for Caris to make a move, but there's no rule that says I can't take the reins.

When I reach for her, she doesn't flinch or pull away. She smiles. Not her usual blithe response, but something genuine.

That smile pushes me forward. When my lips find hers, she wraps her arms around me, nudging me closer. Her hair flows like silk between my fingers.

And when we part, our good-bye feels like practice for our final farewell.

CHAPTER EIGHTEEN

Rabbit fur, gray-blue feathers, mushrooms, chunks of clay, and moldy moss line the countertop in a mishmash that would turn any kitchen clean freak into a nauseous mess. Knife in hand, I try my best at mincing a large green leaf. The pungent smell of rotting nature wafts from the cutting board. Caris pours half a gallon of distilled water into my parents' largest pot, and I feel like a little girl playing at witchcraft.

"Have you ever done this before?" I ask.

Caris clicks on the gas stove. "Made the Purge? No, but I mostly know what I'm doing."

I hope we can finish by the time my parents come home.

"Does the Purge last long in the fridge? It's spring break, and outside of school, I don't make it a point to get near Jasmine."

"We could just knock on her door. She might answer. Then we can shoot an arrow into her and take off running."

"Glorious plan," I say sarcastically.

"So, tell me a better idea. I'm all ears."

I don't have Jasmine's number, and I've never sent her a message on social media. Considering Caris's aversion to the iron in phones, I doubt Raven would answer even if I called or texted. As far as I know, Jasmine's life consists of school, her now ex-boyfriend, a few parties, and tennis.

"Since we're on vacation, Jasmine is either on a trip or working double-time for tennis. If we're lucky, she's practicing every day at the tennis club. We could corner her after practice. That is, if Raven is sticking to Jasmine's daily schedule."

Caris drops the ingredients into the boiling water, one by one. "If Raven is hoping to corner you through Jasmine, then she would try to keep doing whatever Jasmine would normally do. Raven can't trap you if Jasmine is vacationing or holed up at home."

A sharp crash bangs against the front door. Louder than a knock, louder than a package being dropped off. Caris meets my eyes. Hers are full of the same shock that slices through my lungs. Without a word, she heads to the entryway. I follow close behind and flip on the porch light. By the time I consider grabbing the baseball bat that Dad keeps in the umbrella rack, Caris throws the door open.

No one is there, but a pink tennis racket lies askew on the porch mat. Caris steps onto the porch, staring down the driveway. I pick up the racket. There's a rolled-up piece of paper tied to the grip. The page is torn, like it's been ripped from a journal or a book. It's a school directory page, with my name and address. A note is scrawled at the bottom in handwriting I don't recognize: *You can't hide behind that princess forever.*

"Looks like Jasmine is still in town," Caris says. "And Raven knows where you live."

I lean against the wall for support. The racket is shaking, or my hands are trembling, but I can't be sure of either. Caris reaches for my shoulder, but before she can speak, my parents' car pulls into the driveway. The headlights outline Caris's silhouette, bright but blinding.

My brain slowly kicks into gear. Raven is out there, somewhere, possibly watching us from the shadows. But my parents are home, and there's a pot full of sludge in the kitchen.

I shove Raven's note into my pocket. "We have to clean up before my parents come inside," I say.

Caris doesn't hesitate. As she dives into the hallway, I slam the door shut behind us. Back in the kitchen I throw a rag at Caris and shout, "Clean!"

As she hastily scrubs the counter and cutting board with the rag, I grab a plastic container from the cabinet. By the time I finish scooping the Purge in the container, my parents' key clanks in the door lock.

I push the container into Caris's arms. "Hide that in my room."

She laughs at my panic, which weirdly makes me laugh, too. I'm laughing at everything, at the fact that I'm hiding a faerie potion from my parents, at the ridiculousness of a death note tied to Jasmine's pink tennis racket, at the pathetic reality that I'm fighting a threat that no one can see. I laugh as Caris dashes down the hall, but once she disappears around the corner, the laughter dies.

By the time my parents enter the house, I'm scouring the pot with steel wool. Mom and Dad peek into the kitchen. I switch on the garbage disposal and pray that they won't ask me why I was cooking with our largest pot.

"What were you and Caris doing on the porch?" Dad says. "You left your tennis racket out there."

I grab the towel Caris was using to clean and quickly toss it in the cabinet under the sink. "Caris was helping me practice for a bit. I must have forgotten the racket when I brought the tennis balls in."

"I didn't know you have a pink racket," Mom says. Her cheeks are red, which means she's probably had a few glasses of wine.

"I borrowed it from a teammate a long time ago and forgot to give it back." Thank God I'm not a faerie. Thank God I can lie.

"You should return that," Dad says sternly.

I nab a fresh towel from a drawer and start toweling off the pot. "Yeah, sure. I'll return it after spring break."

Neither of them seems up for an interrogation after their date night. After dropping Jasmine's racket on the dining room table, they leave to change out of their dinner clothes and shower. Once their door shuts, I hang the pot on the rack and hurry to my room.

Caris is sitting on my bed, the Purge in plain sight on her lap.

"I said to hide that!" I remind her.

She shrugs. "I would have if it sounded like your parents were coming toward your room."

"I don't know what I would have told them if they found all that stuff in the kitchen."

"Working on a science experiment?"

I roll my eyes. "I thought you couldn't lie."

"I wasn't lying. I was just inspiring you to lie."

"You should get out of here. My parents have been lenient about us doing homework together, but hanging out in my room all night is probably not okay in their book."

"I'm not sure I understand the difference." She hops off the bed and sets the Purge on my nightstand. "Let's finish what we've started, and then I'll go. Also, do you have any iron?"

"I thought we weren't going to burn Jasmine?"

"We aren't. The iron is for your protection. I placed marigolds around your house to deter Wolf, but if Raven could get close enough to throw a tennis racket at your door, I'll need to get some more tonight. While I'm gone, you should keep iron against your window as a security measure."

I'd put iron at every door and window, but my parents wouldn't take kindly to that. As I head out of the room, Caris retrieves a gold arrow from her knapsack. I'm curious, but I'd rather get the iron than ask more questions. In the garage, I find a pair of Dad's dumbbells, a hammer, and a handful of nails. Hopefully, that'll be enough.

By the time I return to my room, Caris is dipping the arrow into the Purge. I line my arsenal of iron on the windowsill. Caris glances over and nods, which I take as confirmation that I'm protected till she collects more marigolds.

"Keep the arrow here tonight," she says. "Just in case. I'll return tomorrow with another arrow and the bow."

The gold arrow gleams in the purple lamplight. "What if Raven is too strong for us?" I ask. "We barely made it past Wolf."

As I remember Wolf's shrieks and the charred skin of his throat, I know that my ability to defeat him hinged more on luck than any real skill. Taking down Raven with a potion and an arrow seems too easy. This isn't a game. While she can't kill Caris, she can torture me to death without any remorse or repercussions.

In a breath, Caris crosses the room to me. Her hands catch my shoulders, so there's no way she can't feel how I'm shaking.

"Truthfully," she says, "you're strong enough to take on the fae. Faeries underestimate humans, but there are reasons we hide ourselves instead of starting an all-out war against mortals. The fact that you can see Raven already gives you an upper hand."

"So, we take down Raven. Then what? What am I supposed to do once you're gone? If another Unseelie comes after me, I won't know how to stop them on my own."

Caris tugs me onto the bed. "You're right. Whether or not I wanted this for you, you're a part of our world now. I can't turn back time, and you will always have the Sight. I can't un-involve you."

When she laces her fingers in mine, I squeeze her hand.

"I don't want to un-involve you," she says.

There is concern written in her brows, yet she glides her fingers along the back of my hand so softly that I feel like I might break. She lifts my fingers to her lips and kisses my knuckles. The gentleness in her eyes is unlike anything she has ever shown me before. Now that I've seen it, I will never unsee it.

"I've been summoned to speak with a messenger again tonight," she says. "After I secure your house, I need to answer my Court's call. I'll go hear what news the messenger has to tell me, but I'll also send a message in reply to the Queen. If she wants me to return home, I would rather not go alone. I'm asking you if you would like to join me."

"You want me to come with you?"

She smiles. "Would you accept if you could?"

In my heart, I've been preparing to be left behind. My parents are leaving for Arizona, and even though they've told me I can go with them, I know they'd prefer I had a plan of my own. I don't belong in Arizona. I don't belong in California either. My world has always been full of the fae. My entire life has revolved around seeing what others can't see. Caris is my only anchor.

Now that the choice is laid out in front of me, I am unshakably sure that I want to go with Caris wherever she goes. The Court of Farrow Wood is impossible for me to imagine, but for years now I've survived on one undeniable truth: When I'm with Caris, I can do anything. With Caris, I belong.

"Let's do it," I say. "I'll go with you."

Caris looks relieved. The soft sigh that escapes her mouth confirms for me that she was worried that I'd say no. This is my choice, and I will choose her. With her, I can face any uncertain future.

She traces my cheek with her free hand. "My mother left my father behind without a second thought, and yet I've lived most of my life with humans. I am human myself. I could never forget you."

When she kisses me, it's like I'm feeling her for the first time. After ten years of friendship, the veil of glamour has fallen away.

"Don't leave me, Ashly," she murmurs into my hair, as though I am the one in danger of leaving and never coming back. I thought I was the only one who couldn't let go, but now I know that I hadn't imagined the gentleness I felt in every whisper we shared, the sweetness in every walk home, and the warmth of every night spent in each other's confidence under the covers. All my questions and worries fade away.

I weave my arms around her neck, and she eases me onto the bed. Her palms trail up my shirt, and I shiver as her fingers dance along my spine. All of me wants to melt into her. I press my lips against her throat, my hands against her heart, which beats as fast as mine. Her breath is heavy in my ears. The fear of the unknown falls away, as she holds me tightly against her.

Gently, she cradles me against her body and kisses my neck. "You'll be safe tonight, Ashly. After I meet with the messenger tonight, I'll come back to you in the morning. We'll stop Raven, and we'll find our way."

I nod against the crook of her neck. I believe her. Caris would never lie to me.

"Time for sleep now," she says, and even though I fight to stay in this time and place with her, I can't stop my eyes from fluttering shut.

❖

Caris is gone in the morning. She must have slipped through the front door because the iron on my windowsill is still in place. The gold arrow rests on my nightstand. Her jacket hangs on my closet doorknob. I wish she'd never left. Her voice echoes in my mind, from all the nights in our past when she'd stayed till sunrise: *Good morning, Ashly.*

"Good morning," I say to my empty room.

Caris said she'd come back soon. So, I just have to do what I'm the worst at: be patient.

My legs ache from sleeping in my jeans. I slide off the mattress, strip to my underwear, and grab a white tennis sweatshirt and a pair of pastel sweats from my dresser. The clock on my phone reads 7:43 a.m. It's almost like I'm getting ready for school, except it's spring break, and I've got nowhere to go this early on a Monday.

I tiptoe down the hall to the bathroom. My parents' door is shut. Dad is probably already gone. Mom is most likely fast asleep. Neither of them knows that I'm planning to take down a killer faerie this evening.

After a long shower, I blow-dry my hair and head to the kitchen. Just yesterday, I was cooking up the Purge with Caris. I don't think I'm ready to shoot an arrow into Jasmine, but Caris will be with me. I'm just support.

As I pour cereal into a bowl, Mom rises from the dead and gloomily turns on the coffeemaker. "What's got you up this early?"

"Nothing much," I say. I don't tell her that Caris used some kind of faerie magic to knock me out several hours before my typical bedtime.

"Doing anything today?"

"I'm grounded, remember?"

She sighs. I pour milk into my cereal. Coffee drips into the pot at a painfully slow speed.

"Do you have any homework to work on over the break?" she asks.

"I have another project for government," I say. School-work is my only way out of the house these days. "Can I go to Caris's house later? She said she could help me with it."

"Who's Caris?"

I nearly drop my spoon on the floor. "C'mon, Mom."

"Sorry," she says. "Remind me who she is?"

I scrutinize her as she grabs a mug from the cabinet. She pours a steaming cup of coffee and grabs the milk from the counter where I left it. There's no trace of playfulness on her tired face. I could almost believe she isn't joking around.

"Caris," I say. "My best friend. Since elementary school."

"I guess you don't talk about her much."

"Tim and Tina's daughter," I insist.

She frowns. "That's not funny, Ashly. You know that Tim and Tina can't have children. Don't make jokes at their expense."

"I'm not."

An anxious look flickers across Mom's face, like when I told her a faerie trashed the locker room. Like when she begged me to swear that I don't see faeries in exchange for extra tennis lessons.

"Are you feeling all right, honey?"

"I'm fine," I say against the lump rising in my throat.

I take my cereal to my room, but I'm not hungry anymore, so I leave it on my nightstand next to the arrow. Caris's jacket is on the doorknob where I left it. I reach out and touch the worn material, if only to make sure that it's real.

There's no way Mom doesn't know who Caris is. She must be messing with me. She must be so fed up with me that she's finally cracked.

I grab a tote bag from my closet. After I toss my phone, wallet, and the arrow inside, I head out of the room. Just because Mom wants to play games doesn't mean I have to go along with it.

"I'm going to get Caris's help on that project," I shout, and shut the front door behind me before she can protest.

It's not even 10:00 a.m. yet, but Caris will just have to forgive me for not waiting around. I rush down the street, through the orchard, and straight to Caris's house. Maybe Mom just drank too much wine last night, or maybe she's having fun pulling a sick joke. Who knows? She and Dad might have conjured a bizarre plan to force me to come to terms with Caris going to college.

A few seconds after I ring the bell, Tim answers the door. His grin is wide as a football. Relief floods my veins. It's the same old Tim, the one who is always happy to welcome his daughter's best friend into his home.

"Hi there, Ashly," he says. His grin doesn't falter, but there are no wrinkles around his eyes. His smile doesn't move past his cheekbones. "What brings you here today? No school?"

"It's spring break," I say, even though he should already know that there's no school this week. Caris hasn't been spending much time at home, but her parents would still be aware of vacation days.

"Is that so? Free as a bird, then. Would you like to come inside for a bit?"

He leads me to the living room. The same rooster artwork hangs on the walls. The bowl of fake fruit sits on the coffee table next to a box of chocolate snack cakes. I take a seat on the paisley-print couch where I've sat beside Caris for years.

"Let me get Tina," he says. "She loves whenever you come to visit."

Once he leaves, I stand back up and reach for the picture frames on the entertainment center. There's a photo of Tim and Tina smiling on a beach in Hawaii. A snapshot of their trip to Paris, the tip of the Eiffel Tower in the background. A candid picture of the two of them laughing at a Thanksgiving dinner. I've heard complaints of these travel stories and family gatherings from Caris, but there's something missing from each of these photographs. Caris isn't anywhere to be seen.

I wander to the stairs. Her senior portrait and eighth grade graduation photo should be hanging on the wall. Instead, a large painting of a sunset on the beach fills the space.

"What a surprise!" Tina says from the top of the stairs. She wears the same smile as Tim, wide and full of teeth, but there's no joy in her eyes. "Tim tells me it's spring break. How thoughtful of you to pay us a visit."

"I thought I'd ask Caris for help with my homework."

Confusion strikes both their faces. "Does Caris live nearby?" Tim asks as they descend the stairs.

"There are lots of Hackley students in the neighborhood," Tina adds. "You're the only one who comes by to say hello, though. Your parents are always talking about you when we cross paths."

My breath swirls in my ears. I barely make it back to the couch against my swimming vision. Tim and Tina keep chatting away with their sad eyes and frozen smiles. *You know Tim and Tina can't have children.* Their miracle child, Caris, is gone without a trace. I don't have to go to her room to know that it's empty—an office or a guest room in its place.

"Would you like a cake?" Tina offers.

I unwrap the plastic with hands that feel detached from my body. The chocolate crumbles in my mouth and scratches my throat. I can hear their conversation, but my brain barely latches onto the words.

"Sometimes the house gets so quiet," Tina says. "It's always nice whenever someone drops by. Hopefully we can take another trip soon."

I nod. Tim says something about visiting an old college buddy in Colorado. The plastic wrapper crinkles in my fingers, and I realize I'm tearing it to bits. The clock on the wall ticks closer to noon. Caris told me she'd come get me in the morning, so why would Tim and Tina forget her? Why would Mom forget her? My hands are shaking, so I close them into fists around the torn plastic. I squeeze my nails into my palm as I try to hold tightly to something, anything, if only so the tears clawing at the backs of my eyes won't fall.

"Are you doing okay, kid?" Tim asks.

My tongue is too heavy to form a fake *I'm fine*. Behind the concern on Tim's face rests an irreparable vacancy. But everyone should remember Caris, because she is supposed to be coming back. Unless she changed her mind. She could have returned to my home in the morning, taken one look at me while I was still fast asleep, and then left forever.

"You said you were on your way to see a friend named Caris?" Tina asks quietly.

I can't tell them that Caris is gone. That there's no one for me to see. That it's like she was never here at all.

CHAPTER NINETEEN

The walk home takes twice as long as it should. As I drag my feet through the orchard, I keep hoping that Caris will jump out from behind one of the trees. She'll say, "You just couldn't wait, could you?" But there's only the buzzing of insects and the rattling of branches to accompany me. As I approach my house, I curse myself for hoping that Caris will be waiting at the mailbox. I cross the front yard, wind around the house, and peek through my window. Of course my bed is empty.

I could cry. I could throw myself into my bedroom, lock the door, and hide behind the iron on my windowsill. I could tell myself that I'll get over this. I could pretend that I never knew someone named Caris.

But I have an arrow in my tote bag, a dark elf out to kill me, and an enemy to save.

At least I think Jasmine needs saving. At this rate, I could go all the way to the tennis club only to discover that Raven disappeared alongside Caris. For all I know, all the faeries are gone. Or my Sight could be gone. I could never have had the Sight at all.

I head back to the street and straight for Kit Park. The sun beats down on the sidewalks and bites against my arms and legs. I wind up walking in circles until I completely lose track of time, but my stomach is finally untangling. As the knots come untied, I realize that a few bites of cereal and a chocolate snack cake aren't sufficient to cover the number of steps I've hit today. I'll die of starvation before Raven gets the chance to off me.

I plod over to the park bathroom next to Kit Playground. There's a pair of vending machines for snacks and sodas. I feed the machines several dollar bills and select some mixed nuts, a granola bar, and a red Gatorade. With my makeshift meal in tow, I settle down on a bench that faces the playground.

Since it's spring break, there's a record number of children climbing on the jungle gym. Parents and older siblings line the rubber turf. I don't recognize any Hackley students. The giant snake sculpture looms nearby, and a toddler is playing peekaboo with her mother behind its curvy body. No one is here alone. Except me.

It's funny how hunger takes over the brain, pushing out all the other thoughts. Once I've finished the granola bar and half the nuts, the gravity of my situation takes full control. Caris is gone. She completely disappeared, glamouring herself out of everyone's memory. Whether that was her work, or the work of faeries who came to clean up after she went home, or a plan that's always been in place since she arrived, I have no way of knowing. That I still remember her may be a pity move on her part, or a consequence of my Sight.

For all her talk about taking me with her, I'm still here. So much for the fae's inability to lie. Then again, when I comb through our conversation, Caris never promised to take me with her. She only asked if I wanted to come along. I can't even feed myself a story of Caris being caught in the crossfire of some conflict with the Unseelie. They'd signed a treaty that prevented any harm from being done to her.

She said she could never forget me, but that promise is as strong as sand, slipping through my fingers, tossed to the wind. In the end, I'm nothing more than a memory.

I shove down the tears in my throat with a swig of Gatorade. Caris hated red Gatorade. I take another long drink.

For now, I'm on my own, and that means I have to take down Raven by myself while I still have the element of surprise in my favor. Otherwise, she'll shred me the moment I let my guard down. Not to mention what'll happen to Jasmine. The war between the Unseelie, the Seelie, and the Court of Farrow Wood has nothing to do with Jasmine's life. Her future is on the chopping block, and I'm the only one who can help her, because I'm the only one who knows.

I throw my trash in the garbage on the side of the playground. Carson Tennis Club is close enough to already make out in the distance. If Raven isn't there, then it's back to the drawing board. If she is, then there's no going back.

Trying to look as inconspicuous as possible, I bypass the clubhouse. My name is still on their blacklist. A manicured line of trees divides the building from its six tennis courts. As I walk alongside the chain-link fences that enclose each court, I peer inside. My jaw hurts from the stress. I hope to find Raven, and I also hope that she's not here.

There are four older women in one court. A father and son in the next. I cross through the middle of the courts and pray that I don't run into anyone I know. As luck would have it, Lanie is volleying with one of her younger students. The girl has thick curly hair and a strong serve. She looks determined, even though she's probably still in middle school. I must have looked that way once.

Lanie shouts for them to take a break, so I hustle to the next court. If she saw me, she didn't call me out. Maybe she doesn't care to bother with me anymore. What would she say if I told her why I've come here? Even if I succeed in stopping Raven, there won't be any applause. There won't be a high-five or a *well done*. Caris won't be there to say, *I knew you could do it*.

So, I'm doing this for myself. That will have to be enough.

By the time I round the corner to the last court, I'm ready to call it a day. I can try again tomorrow and every day until I find Raven.

But I don't have to wait until tomorrow because there she is. Her dark hair is pulled into her trademark high ponytail. Her white tennis shirt is impeccable, her swings perfect. She's so much like Jasmine that it's hard to believe that there's an evil burning inside her. An evil that's hunting me.

I wait on the grass. Jasmine's instructor's back is to me, so the only one who might see me is Jasmine herself. The practice winds down quickly. They collect the balls around the court, and then her instructor joins her on the other side of the net. His final remarks are reminiscent of the pointers Lanie used to share with me. Jasmine nods a few times as she catches her breath.

"I want to practice a bit more," she says.

"We'll be here tomorrow," he tells her.

"Yeah, I know. I just want a few more minutes to work on my flat serve. You don't have to wait up for me. I'll cool down on my own."

He crosses his arms. "Don't skip the cool-down."

"I won't."

With that, he collects his water bottle and tennis jacket and heads off the court. The sun is beginning to set. Jasmine grabs a ball from the caddy and lifts it into the air. Her grip doesn't match a typical flat serve, and sure enough, she slice-serves the ball. Straight into the fence. Right in front of me.

My blood runs cold. Raven stalks toward me, mouth twisted in a smug smile.

"After all that work the princess went through to shroud your home with marigolds," she says, "you've come here seeking your own death. Mortals never cease to astound me."

While my instincts scream at me to run, I suspect that Raven is hoping to scare me into fleeing. For a faerie, catching a human is probably easier than fighting one hand-to-hand. Yet I can use that to my advantage. If Raven thinks I'm running, then she might lower her guard even more.

I waste no time and sprint toward the woods. An all-out faerie brawl on the tennis court would get me charged for drunken misbehavior anyway. As I run, I reach into my bag and grab the arrow and my phone for its flashlight. While the forest provides me cover, I can't see in the dark, and the sun is setting fast. Nighttime will work in Raven's favor. I can't have it all.

I duck behind a tree. There's no rustling. The animals and fae have hushed, as if frightened into reverent silence by Raven's arrival, but I can't make her out in the shadows, and I don't want to risk the flashlight yet.

"Hiding is futile," she calls out. The iciness in her voice is beyond anything Jasmine could conjure. "Why hide? Accepting your fate will make things much easier."

I hope she keeps talking. Then I can measure how far she is from me, but there's nothing more but silence and waiting. I grip the arrow tighter in my hand. Without Caris's bow, I'll have to get closer to Raven. If I can trip her up, then I might get an opening to stab her. Even then, I have to be careful not to drive the arrow into her heart or her throat, or else Jasmine might die. And no one would believe me if I told them that I'd been trying to exorcise a faerie from Jasmine's body. Her murder would fall on my head.

A soft wind blows through the trees. The scratching of wood and leaves swirls around me. I glance up and around, but Raven is nowhere to be seen. I'm almost impatient for her to find me, but I regret that thought the moment her cold fingers grab my arm.

I tear away and raise the arrow, but she jumps back and lands a few feet away. A sickening cackle fills my ears.

"An arrow?" she says. "What are you planning to do with that, little mortal?"

"Come closer and find out," I say.

"Where is your princess now? The war is over, and she has forsaken you. I heard that the Court of Farrow Wood is celebrating the end of the war tonight. Your human life is nothing. Even though your death is meaningless to her, I have my brother's pride to avenge."

I need to focus, but her words about Caris sting more than her threats. Caris is celebrating, dancing and laughing with the elves in her Court, while I'm here, left to fend for myself against her foe. The Caris I know was flighty and carefree, but I never thought she would throw me to the wind. That she would abandon me. Yet she has done just that.

Raven pounces toward me. Her nails come for my throat, but I backpedal and dodge her just in time. A fallen branch trips up my foot. I nearly crash to the ground, but a nearby tree catches my fall. There's no more sun, only darkness at every corner. I switch on my phone flashlight, but Raven is nowhere to be seen. The trees block my line of sight.

This won't do, so I make a run for it. If I can find a clearing, then I can even the playing field.

My flashlight pierces the night. I point it to the forest floor, jumping over debris and fallen logs. A branch slaps my face, knocking me backward and straight into Raven.

She grasps for my throat once more. As her fingers wind around my neck, my lungs catch fire. Panic seizes my entire body. I would scream, but all sound is suffocated out of me.

With all the strength I can muster, I raise the arrow, but Raven is fast. She knocks the arrow from my hand with her free arm. Still, even that small move distracts her just enough. I thrust my foot into her knee. She screeches, releases me, and drops to the forest floor writhing.

The fresh oxygen in my lungs does little to relieve my terror. If I lose the arrow, I've lost everything. In a frenzy, I drop to the ground. The arrow has to be somewhere within the fallen leaves and muddy holes. When my flashlight finally glints on gold, I crawl toward it desperately and grasp the arrow as quickly as I spring to my feet. I'm not sticking around for Raven to catch me after she recovers.

My lungs have no choice but to come back to life as I dash toward what I hope is a clearing in the distance. I break through the line of trees. In the center there's a hill, and the crescent moon shines weakly on the waving grass. Caris guided me here twice before. We shared a picnic in this same spot. Several weeks later, she revealed her true self to me. Now, no matter where I look, I will never see her again.

The common fae gather round in the forest of the night. Their eyes burn brightly in the distance. There's a show tonight, something new to capture their attention. My death would be but a passing amusement in their eternal lives.

I shine my flashlight at those many eyes. Amongst the shadows, a pair of frigid blue irises peers back. Raven steps forward, limping lightly. I grip the arrow tighter. One prick is all it takes.

"The Unseelie already lost the war," I say. "No one likes a sore loser."

"The war may be over," Raven hisses, "but your head will be a prize, mounted to my wall."

This time, when she lunges at me, I have the arrow ready. I side shuffle and aim straight for her right arm. Jasmine is right-handed, and that knowledge paralyzes me for a moment. With a single stab, I could save Jasmine from Raven and shatter her entire tennis career.

My hesitation destroys my momentary advantage. Raven throws her whole weight toward me, sinking her nails straight into my abdomen. But in doing so, she's completely open. I jab the arrow into her left shoulder. The struggle is finally over. I've won. Unless the Purge fails me. If this doesn't work, then I'm as good as dead.

Raven glances to the arrow still stuck in the miniscule wound I've inflicted and laughs. "Is that all you can do? Pathetic."

When she withdraws her claws from my stomach, I crumple to the ground. Pain slices through me, pinning me down, stirring up vomit that I barely manage to swallow.

But then Raven begins coughing. It starts small, like she's clearing her throat, but gradually worsens into wheezing. Doubling over, she tears at her shoulder. She rips the arrow from her skin and throws it at my feet.

"What have you done?" she sputters.

She drops to her knees as her face contorts into a mask of pure agony. Her mouth falls open, seeking air or trying to scream, but no sound comes out. Instead, a dense shadow pours forward. It pools onto the grass and slithers toward me like a snake raring to bite. But I'm out of ideas. I don't know how to take down a shadow without light, and my flashlight is yards away.

"What is this?" the shadow howls. "You—nothing but mortal trash. What have you done to me?"

Just as suddenly as the shadow took shape, it halts and curls into a ball. The ball shrinks, smaller and smaller, until it's only a dot. Until there's nothing there at all. Just as Caris said: The Purge would force Raven out of Jasmine's body, and then she'd retreat.

I can only hope that she never returns.

My stomach throbs. Warm blood floods from my abdomen. My fingers find a gaping wound where Raven's fingers stabbed me. A wave of dizziness threatens to overtake me. But if I lie down here, I'll die. By the time a search party finds my body, there won't be enough blood left to keep my heart beating.

Surviving on adrenaline alone, I throw Jasmine's arm over my shoulder. The faeries' eyes glow in the dark. They could help us, but the thought probably never occurs to them.

Instead, they watch as two humans slowly drag their way through the woods.

I stumble out of the trees and onto the grass. With my last ounce of strength, I carry Jasmine toward the floodlight of the tennis club. We make it to the fence of the court where this all began. I lower her to the ground. Her skin is cold, but her chest heaves.

At least she's breathing is all I can think. At least I've done something right. My fingers find my stomach, which is wet and throbbing with pain. The pain buckles my knees. My cheek hits the tennis court fence, and then I'm falling down, farther than I've ever fallen before.

CHAPTER TWENTY

When I wake up, there is no tennis court. There are no trees or grass. Jasmine isn't nearby, and I can't make out whether it's day or night. Fuzz fills my vision, but I shake off the vertigo. Across the room, there's a whiteboard with numbers written under my name. A green line bounces across the screen of a heart monitor. When I try to touch my stomach, a thin tube pulls at my arm where it's taped to my skin.

I lean into the elevated hospital bed. It could be worse than this. I could be dead.

The door creaks shut. The outline of a visitor wavers in the dim light, only a few feet away. By the way that the figure stands perfectly still, I know that it's not human. I blink away the dizziness and make out eyes darker than the midnight sky. She is taller than before and pointed ears slice through her dark hair. Even so, there is no denying who she is.

"Always the impatient one," Caris says.

She wheels a chair over to the side of my bed and sits so casually you'd think she's been here time and time again. Her neck is bare. The pendant she's worn since I met her is long gone, and now I can see her for who she is. Part human, part fae. She is beautiful in a way that distances her from others.

"Where have you been?" I ask. Drowsiness laces each of my words, like I'm drunk. Like I'm only half-awake.

"A little bit here and a little bit there."

I reach out to smack her, but the IV line snags. A sharp pang knifes through my stomach. Bandages peek out from beneath my papery hospital shirt. Caris stares at the bandages, too.

"You could have waited," she says. "At least a day or two."

"I thought you'd gone home. No one remembered you. It was like you'd disappeared completely. Tim and Tina don't even have any photos of you anymore."

"How are they?" she asks.

I could tell her the painful truth, that the single most joy in Tim and Tina's life has been carved out by a blade they never saw coming. "They miss you, but they don't know what it is that they're missing. Other than that, I guess they're okay."

"With more time, they'll feel better," she says, but I can't tell if she's trying to convince me or herself. "Their residual emotions will fade."

"It's like you disappeared completely."

"But you remembered me."

Her gaze is unbearably deep, as if a riddle wades in its wake, but I'm too tired to solve anything. I'm too angry to play any games.

"What's a memory worth when you've been left behind to fend for yourself?" I say.

She closes her eyes, then slowly opens them as that sly grin appears on her lips. "I heard news that Raven had run back to the Unseelie, wounded and ashamed. So I came to see how you fared."

"How does it look like I fared?"

She chuckles. "It looks like you won."

"No thanks to you."

"I shouldn't be here yet," she says. "I have a few more details to iron out. The Queen has a way of making things difficult."

"Sounds like a faerie problem."

She trails her hand down my arm, and I have half a mind to shrug her off. But the feel of her fingers, solid and sure on my skin, is something I can't refuse. Because it's what I've missed. It's what I thought I lost.

"Why did you leave?" I ask.

"I didn't choose to leave. I was summoned home by the Queen. With the war over and the treaty confirmed, there was nothing tethering me to the mortal world anymore. Or so the Queen said. That was the message I went to collect that night."

So then, while faeries can't lie, they can't predict the future either. When Caris said she was going to collect news from a messenger, she might not have known that the news would be a command to go home.

"By returning to the Court of Farrow Wood, I fulfilled my oath to the Queen," she adds. "Now that I'm free, I've got another promise to keep."

"What promise is that?"

"Don't tell me you've forgotten?" She smiles gently and takes my hand. "You said you would come with me to the Court of Farrow Wood. Or have you changed your mind?"

My heart trembles in my chest, but as my blood races, my stomach aches even more. It hurts, but it also feels like hope. "You left me," I say. I'm not ready to forgive her yet.

Softly, she kisses my shoulder. "I didn't mean to. And I'm back. Besides, besting an Unseelie on your own is sure to earn you a place in the faerie kingdom. Although I've always known that you are not like other mortals. You're not like the faeries either. To me, you are so much more."

Her words, warm as the sun breaking through a canopy of trees, quiet all my pain. "You could apologize," I say with half-hearted resistance.

"I could. But I'll save that for another day and another misunderstanding. For now, try not to anger any more fae. I'll come back to get you soon."

She releases my hand and heads to the door. I could let

her go, and wallow in self-pity and doubts, but with a faerie, there's a better way.

"Wait," I say.

She peers over her shoulder. She waits.

"Swear to me that you'll come back."

If she can make an oath to the Queen that kept her in the mortal world for ten years, then hopefully a promise can tie her to me, too. Or she could walk out the door. The choice is hers.

"Ashly Harris," she says. "I swear that we will be together in the Court of Farrow Wood."

That's better than any oath I could have come up with. I really need to practice my faerie language skills.

The door opens, and a nurse walks in, right past Caris, without a single glance in her direction. He hustles to my side with a grin. "You're awake," he says.

From behind the nurse, Caris waves. The nurse can't see her. She'll step into the hallway and out of the hospital, and not a single person will know she's been here. No one except me. I wish that they could see her.

"Are you really here?" I ask Caris.

But either she doesn't hear me, or she doesn't think I'm speaking to her, because she walks out the door without another word.

"Yeah, I'm here, and you're okay," the nurse says. "Your parents will be so happy to see you. They just went to the cafeteria to get coffee and a little dinner."

I'm not ready to talk to my parents. I'm too tired to lie. If only I could tell them everything that's happened and what I've managed to overcome, then maybe I could make them proud for once. But the truth is that who I am is not who they need me to be. No matter how much they love me, I will never become normal. I can only pretend.

So, I fake being asleep. It's almost like glamour. When they walk into the room, they see their sleeping daughter, but really, I'm awake and aware and so sorry that they can't see what's right in front of them.

❖

The nurses tell me that I underwent surgery on my stomach for stab wounds. They say that I can leave in a few days if I continue to heal well. My dizziness is the effect of a heavy dose of painkillers. Apparently, the police are still looking for the person who attacked me and Jasmine. They'll be looking for the rest of their lives.

I've resigned myself to hours of boredom and thumbing through social media posts of other people's epic spring break excursions. Mom bought me a few magazines, but fashion and tennis articles get old real fast. It's pretty sad when the highlight of your day is a tray of mushy hospital food. Sometimes the nurses sneak me Sprite, even though the carbonation isn't the best for a torn-up stomach. Somehow that makes the soda taste even better.

I'm in between a daydream and a daytime television show when the thwack of flip-flops enters my room. Jasmine hovers in the doorway. Her perfectly made-up face stands in sharp contrast to the sling that holds her left arm.

"Are you up for a visit?" she asks. One foot is in the room, the other over the threshold. I could kick her out.

We've never had much to say to each other outside of snide remarks and middle fingers. But I switch off the TV and gesture toward the chair at my bedside. The last time we spoke, Raven had full control over her. Even if our conversation turns into ugly accusations, I'd be relieved to have things go back to normal.

She takes a seat. "I've been out of the hospital since yesterday," she says. "My instructor is pissed about my arm, but he's trying to hide it. Brad wanted me to bring you this."

She takes a get-well card out of her bag. There isn't much

inside, only a generic card greeting and his signature. I place it next to the flowers my parents brought me. I never thought I'd get sentimental about hospital gifts, but the card looks good on the table. It means that someone other than my family gave me a second thought.

"Brad wants to know if he can come by and see you," Jasmine says. "He didn't want to stress you out or anything. Funny that I'm the one passing along the message."

In other words, she's worried that I don't want her here. But she's the only one who might know the truth about what happened to us. I need to know what she remembers. Everyone keeps asking me questions, and the police even interrogated me about that night. I struggled to keep my comments vague. Hopefully, the cops chalked it up to trauma and painkillers.

"How bad is your arm?" I ask.

She shrugs, then winces a little. "The doctors say that I can start physical therapy in a week. I'll be back on the court in a month. That's what I'm telling myself anyway."

"That's good." I'm glad I managed to stab her in the shoulder of her left arm. When tennis is your whole life, losing the ability to play is soul-crushing. I know this, and I wouldn't wish that on anyone. Not even the person who almost stole tennis from me in middle school.

"I was hoping that you have an idea of what happened the other night," Jasmine says. "I can't remember much. I was practicing at Carson, and then everything went blank. I'd been blacking out for a while, but I thought it was stress. I'd hoped it would go away on its own, and it did after the Carson custodial staff found us outside the tennis court, but I don't know what happened. One moment I was on the court, the next I was lying on the ground, covered in your blood."

"You wouldn't believe me if I told you," I say, because it's true, and because I'm tired of playing dumb.

Jasmine rubs her fingers along her sling. There are a few

signatures there, most likely from her friends. No one has signed my stomach bandages. Not that I'd want them to.

"But I think I would believe you," she says. "I believed you back in the seventh grade. You said that a faerie threw everyone's tennis gear and clothes in the shower. I didn't see a faerie, but I didn't see you do it either. You were with me the whole time. Demons and angels and faeries and all that spiritual stuff—it's so out there that it has to be made-up. That's what I told myself, but someone tried to kill us, Ashly. You could have died, and I can't even remember what happened after I picked up tennis balls with my instructor."

I don't owe Jasmine an explanation. I already saved her from Raven, and that should be enough. But she's terrified, and she'll have questions hanging over her head for the rest of her life.

"What if I told you that we took a walk in the woods to hash things out?" I say. "Then someone appeared out of nowhere with a knife. We took off running, but we got slashed up, and once we got out of the woods, the guy backed off."

"Sounds believable, but I don't believe you."

I sigh. "And you would believe me if I told you that we were attacked by an evil faerie?"

"I'm not sure. All I know is that there are black feathers in my bedroom, and I don't own a bird."

That actually makes me laugh, which hurts my stomach like hell. The painkillers must be wearing off. Without the drugs to keep me calm, the anger begins to creep in. It starts small, a whisper that wants Jasmine to go. Then it grows big enough to make me want to shove her out. After all these years, Jasmine wants an explanation. So I give her one.

"You and I are completely different," I say. "You said so yourself. You have tennis and college and enough friends to lose some and still feel good. But you still found the time to push me down and make me feel small. Everyone wanted me to be small and follow the rules and be easy, but I've never been small. You can believe what you want and take that with you out the door."

Jasmine rises out of the chair. Looming over me, she looks like she has half a mind to argue. I may be lying in a hospital bed, but I'm ready to fight. Then she takes a deep breath and sits back down.

"I never thought you were small," she says. "You had talent in everything that I had to work twice as hard to do. I lied in seventh grade because my parents were always comparing me to you. Coach would point out your strengths and tell me to measure up. To be honest, Ashly, I was jealous of you."

Envy has a sneaky way of destroying things. Hearing Jasmine's confession stings, if only because I would never have the guts to tell her that I want what she has, too. A world where her gifts are recognized and encouraged. A life that others deem purposeful. A future where people cheer her on.

"Your slice serve is better than mine," I say.

She smiles. "Thanks."

We sit in silence for a while, for long enough to feel both awkward and remorseful. If Jasmine had backed me up in seventh grade, we might still be on the same team. There might be an alternate universe where we're friends, walking the same path, still playing doubles.

But the only person I have is Caris, and Caris is an empty space in everyone else's memory. I'm not even sure if she visited me in the hospital, or if the painkillers made me dream what I wanted most.

"Do you remember Caris?" I ask, even though I'm setting myself up for pain.

Jasmine's brows furrow. She has a lot of missing memories right now, after all. "Who is Caris?" she asks.

"No one. Never mind."

She nods. "I'll see you back at school?" she asks. "No more fights in the quad, okay?"

"It's a deal."

When she leaves, I switch the TV back on. A local car dealership commercial flashes on the screen. A salesman walks down a line of luxury vehicles. No one sees the sprite on the hood of a red convertible. If I'm the only one who sees it, does that make me the wiser? Or am I just a girl with a problem? If Caris never returns, at some point I'll have to come to terms with the fact that I need help.

A gentle knock pulls me away from the commercial break. This time, it's Dad. I'm wide awake, so there's no way out of this conversation. He sits in the same chair that Jasmine occupied only minutes before. He has a bag in his hand, but I doubt there's any more cards for me.

"Hey, kid," he says quietly. "Glad to see you're up. I thought you might want a few things from home to cheer you up."

He hands me the bag. I fish out my laptop, a childhood teddy bear that I kept on my desk, and a family photo from Christmas two years ago. At the bottom is a folded-up jean jacket.

"How are you feeling today, Ashly?" he asks.

I'm angry, I want to say, but as I spread Caris's jacket across my lap, I know that it's not true. The anger has always been a front. I'm lonely. The tears I've worked so hard to hide spill down my cheeks so hot they could burn. I wish they would burn me. Then I could be mad about something. But I'm trapped by the questions I'm not allowed to ask. I'm alone.

CHAPTER TWENTY-ONE

The doctors have cleared me to leave. I'm supposed to celebrate. Sure, I'm tired of the hospital bed, bored of the food choices, and annoyed by the well-meaning nurses' grins, but I've still got a gash that's going to take months to heal. As I sit on the chair in my hospital room, I sift through the hefty discharge papers. There are checklists for everything: bathing, redressing the wound, even going to the bathroom. Dad is chatting with the doctor about the details, but most of the aftercare is going to fall on my shoulders. I'm the one who needs to be careful every time I shower and double-check that the skin around the wound hasn't turned green in the morning.

"Ready to go, Ashly?" Dad says, like I have a choice in the matter. I shrug and tentatively rise from the chair. A wheelchair waits for me at the door. I roll my eyes but don't complain. Even though I'm the one who dressed myself this morning, the hospital doesn't want to take any chances. A slip and fall on my way out is a lawsuit waiting to happen.

A cheery nurse wheels me down the hall. Dad walks by my side, one eye still on his copy of the discharge papers. He looks concerned but keeps his worries to himself. We pass a bustling reception desk, wait for the elevator, and navigate around nurses and visitors. Between all the hustle and bustle, there's an emptiness that only I seem to notice. Not once in these past ten days have I seen a single faerie.

I guess the fae would rather wreak havoc than hang out with the wounded and dying. Can't say I blame them.

The nurse takes her leave at the exit. "You're a trouper, Ashly," she says. "You'll be all better in no time."

Dad thanks her, and then it's just the two of us and my first sip of fresh air since my dance with death in the forest. The car is parked at the curbside pickup. Instead of wheeling me that way, Dad offers me a hand.

"Wanna walk?" he asks.

I take his hand and wobble to two feet. He smiles at me but doesn't turn toward the car. I could smile back, but my stomach stings, and suddenly, more than ever, I want to go home.

"What is it?" I say.

"Just looking at you," he says. "You know, when your mom and I got the call that you were in the emergency room, I thought for a second that my heart was going to stop. They said there'd been an accident. Some kind of attack. I had a thousand questions running through my mind, but the first one I asked was, *Is she going to be okay?* And look at you, Ashly."

He pulls me into a hug, so sudden that I gasp. "You're my little girl," he says. "My little girl fought off the worst kind of person, all by herself. You scare me almost every day, Ashly, but you amaze me every day, too. You're a fighter. I'm proud that my daughter is a fighter."

I nearly tell him to stop hugging me. I could use my stomach as an excuse and say he's hurting me. But the weight of his arms around my shoulders and the heat of his palms on my back draw me in. I can't remember the last time Dad hugged me, and I have no memories of him sharing that he's proud of me. So, I don't move. I lean into the whirlpool of emotions swirling in my chest. I breathe in this moment for as long as I can, and when we finally step away, I hold on to his words. We step into the car, and I squeeze my arms where he held me.

Ten days ago, I took down Raven. I fought off a nightmare and saved Jasmine. No one knows what really happened, but it doesn't matter for once. Even if no one understands me, they can still see that I did the right thing. I'm not the villain. I never was.

❖

When Dad pulls into the driveway, we're met by a welcoming party. The gnomes are swaying on the porch swing, waving to the car. The common fae would almost be cute if they weren't so invasive.

Mom is cooking in the kitchen. The same pot Caris and I used for the Purge sits on the stove. "I made chicken and vegetable soup for when you're hungry," she says before wrapping me in a light hug. "I'm so glad you're finally home."

Dad tacks a list on the fridge of all the foods I should and shouldn't eat while my stomach heals. Basically, I'm stuck eating like Caris. No junk food or artificial flavors for a long while. I guess there are consequences for battling a dark elf.

"I'll be in my room," I say, mostly because I'm exhausted. All I've done today is get discharged and go home, yet I already need a nap.

My bedroom is painfully familiar. Same purple lamps, same double bed. The hammer and nails and dumbbells still guard the window, but the Purge is no longer on the nightstand. Thankfully, Mom and Dad were too upset about my hospitalization to ask any questions about my science experiment.

Without bothering to change clothes, I burrow beneath the blankets. I don't know when I fall asleep, but when my eyes blink open, it's already dark. The stench of hospital antiseptic smothers me. I lift the sleeve of Caris's jean jacket to my nose, and sure enough, it reeks from all the days I never took it off.

Stepping out of my room, I find myself alone in the pitch-black hallway. Once my eyes adjust, I can make out my parents' bedroom door, cracked open only a fraction of an inch. They usually shut their door at night, and I can't help but wonder if they kept it cracked for me, like I might wake from a bad dream and come crawling under their covers.

I switch on a lamp in the living room, and the clock reads 2:10 a.m. It's an odd time to start a load of laundry, but I'm wide awake from my long nap. The cold tile of the laundry room floor sends a shiver up my spine. The chill almost makes me turn back, but I need to wash Caris's jacket if I plan to wear it again.

I gingerly peel off the jacket, careful not to arch my stomach in the process. This is easy, I tell myself. Just put the jacket into the washing machine, add detergent, press the power button. But once the machine lock clicks, a wave of panic crashes over me. The water gushes into the tub. Soon, the jacket will be filled with soap, rinsing every last remnant of Caris from the fiber.

I swear that we will be together in the Court of Farrow Wood, she said, but I have no way of knowing if that was a dream. None of the nurses saw her. Only me. It's always just me that sees the faeries. If a faerie disappears, then it's like they were never there to begin with.

I'm not going to stand by and watch the laundry for the next thirty minutes, but I don't feel like watching TV, and my phone feels miles away in my bedroom. Besides, swiping through photos of Hackley spring break adventures on social media seems less than alluring. I wind up standing in the quiet living room, next to the lamp that Grandma spoke to that night, so many years ago. Nothing moves. I switch off the light, and the streetlamps outside the window cast a shadow from the lamp onto the floor.

The shadow is still as death, and yet I find myself wishing for the inky blackness to shift, to shudder. If the shadow twisted into a new shape, I wouldn't know what to do. If I'm being honest, I'd probably be terrified. But fear might be better than the emptiness—maybe a little. I turn the light back on and settle on the couch. I watch the clock, which isn't any better than watching laundry, but I'm out of ideas.

When the washing machine finally beeps, I pull the jacket out. The scent of lavender wafts from the fabric. The hospital smell is long gone, but so is Caris. I can choose to believe that she came to see me that night. I can hang on to her promise, but I don't know which is harder: waiting for her or letting her go.

Back in my bedroom, I hang the jacket on the handle of my closet door. The fatigue hits me then, returning with a vengeance. But before I turn out the light, I wander over to the window. The pile of iron still rests on the windowsill. Piece by piece, I remove the dumbbells, the hammer, and the nails. On a whim, I open the window. A breeze rolls in, kissing my face with its soft sigh. The wind carries the whisper of pixie laughter from the garden.

I smile into the night. When I finally ease back into bed, I listen for that laughter. Perhaps Caris is laughing now, too, someplace far away, where I can never reach.

CHAPTER TWENTY-TWO

Heading back to school after spring break is supposed to feel miserable, but returning after a stomach surgery is a whole lot worse. To add salt to the wound is the fact that I have no one to hang out with in the halls between classes, no one to eat lunch with, no one to text in the bathroom. I hover by my locker before homeroom, sorting through binders that don't need sorting. I'm actually counting down the minutes before the bell rings.

"Ashly!" I whip around, faster than my doctors would like, to see Brad grinning in my direction. He's surrounded by his typical letterman crew, but as they near me, he tells them to go on without him. Cameron makes eye contact with me and waves as he passes by. I nod back. When was the last time someone waved to me at school? Stares, muffled giggles, and averted gazes are the greetings I've come to expect.

"I'm glad you're back," Brad says.

"You're probably the only one," I say without a trace of any real sadness.

"Don't say that. I know Jasmine will be happy to know you're here."

I make a show of reorganizing my textbooks. "How's she doing?" I'm not making small talk. Jasmine had a sling back at the hospital, and while my injuries definitely trump hers, a damaged shoulder is no joke for a tennis player.

"She's holding up. I take her to physical therapy after school sometimes."

Translation: They're back together. I imagine nearly losing your ex-girlfriend to a killer menace in the woods would spur any guy to rekindle a relationship.

"She told me you saved her life," Brad says. "Everyone's been talking about how you kicked a would-be murderer's ass. There's gotta be a graduation award for that."

"I've been vying for that award all my life."

Brad laughs, which makes me smile. Finally tired of pretending to care about the contents of my locker, I shut the door and turn to him.

"Did you get my card?" he asks.

"Yeah, thank you." I hope he can tell that I mean it.

"I didn't know if it would be weird for me to visit you. Jasmine said you were in pretty bad shape." He leans against the lockers and chuckles softly. "Jasmine's really changed since that night. She apologized to me, actually. She said she was sorry for bad-mouthing you all the time. I think she's finally put whatever rivalry you two had going behind her."

I have nothing to say to that. While I'm thankful that Jasmine has really turned over a new leaf, it's not like we'll be trading friendship bracelets anytime soon.

Brad clears his throat. "Anyway, I was worried you would be in the hospital for a long time, but you look the same as when I last saw you. Still, that must have been—"

The warning bell rings. He shrugs and steps away from the lockers.

"Guess that's my cue to go," he says. "Don't be a stranger."

As I watch him saunter off, a twinge of loneliness worms its way through me. It's not like I would have wanted to walk to class together. I'll be moving from class to class by myself from here on out. Now is not the time to start feeling sorry for myself.

So, self-pity isn't the reason I call out to Brad, but I am

relieved that he stops. As he makes his way back toward me, I remember the Brad who lost that touchdown for his team, who got detention in middle school for falling asleep too many times in social studies, who always pushed too hard when we played tag on the playground at recess. We met in the fourth grade, on the same playground where I met Caris. Her jean jacket cocoons me, even now.

"Do you remember Caris?" I ask, even though I'm setting myself up for heartbreak. But maybe there is someone out there who has a single memory of her. If only someone could remember her, then her absence wouldn't be so final.

Brad furrows his brows. "Caris? Did we go to school together?"

A wisp of hope flutters through me. "We did."

"I don't remember her," he says.

The small flicker of hope evaporates in an instant. I shove my hands into the pockets of Caris's jacket and squeeze them into fists, as though I could grab on to something to keep me grounded. But there's only thin air. There is no one to hold my hand. Instead, my nails stab into my palms.

Of course Brad wouldn't remember. He may not be as bad as I'd thought. He might even be nice, and we might wave to each other in the halls from now on, but he can't see faeries. He will always think that I saved Jasmine from a human in the woods, and he'll be better off never knowing the truth.

The final bell rings, which means we're both late for class. "I'll see you later," he says and sprints off.

Sure, I'll see him later, but not for much longer. Brad will go to college, just like Cameron, and just like Jasmine. Hackley High School will be a remnant of the past, a few years of my life that will disintegrate into a handful of memories. After graduation, I'll probably never step foot on this campus again.

I speed-walk down the hall toward homeroom. As I turn a corner, I come face-to-face with a sprite. She sits cross-legged on top of a bench in the quad. She glances my way and waves a lazy, long-fingered hand in my direction. Her gold eyes sparkle in the morning sun.

Even after I graduate, the faeries will be around to wave hello. If I land a job or wind up in college somehow, they'll be there. Once I get a place of my own, the faeries will be peering at me from outside the window. My life may slow down or pick up. Everything can change in an instant, but the faeries will be there. Always have been. Always will be. That I can rely on.

❖

I throw my backpack on my bedroom floor. There's a pile of makeup work stuffed inside. While my teachers told me there's no rush to get it all done, I've never been good at managing my assignments. Falling further behind will only make matters worse.

Mom peeks her head past the door. Since it was my first day back at school, she took the day off work in case of any emergencies. To my surprise, she waves her phone in my direction.

"Grandma wants to chat," she says. "You up for a call?"

Grandma never calls anymore, not since the cancer took over so much of her body. I take the phone without question and hear the crackle of her breath on the other line.

"Hi, Grandma," I say.

"If it isn't little Ashly, all grown up, and out of the hospital," she says.

The huskiness of her voice can't drown out the affection. I close my eyes and imagine her in her worn armchair in Arizona. Her short white hair curls around the wrinkles of her face. Pearl earrings shine in each ear, and a soft smile lights up her blue eyes.

"I'm all right," I say.

Mom gestures down the hall, then heads out of the room and back to whatever show she was watching before Grandma called. I shut the door behind her before taking a seat on the edge of my bed.

"I'm glad to hear that," Grandma says. "You were out in the woods looking for trouble, young girl. The woods are no place for women at night. You should be safe in your bed."

I remember Grandma sending me off to bed as she stood down the shadow on the floor in the living room. She could have run away, too, but she fought instead. Or that could have been a figment of my childhood imagination. I've never asked her, and now, more than ever, I want to know what she sees and has seen.

"It wasn't the safest thing to do," I tell her. "But it all worked out in the end."

"And what made you go looking for danger in the first place?"

The secret I've been harboring begs to break free. "There was a shadow," I say. "And I had to stop it."

Grandma doesn't reply right away, which might mean she thinks I'm out of my mind, or she might hear my words and understand them. "Is that so?" she says. "And did you stop it?"

"I think I did, but I'm the only one who saw the shadow, so I don't know for sure."

A soft chuckle fills my ear. "I would tell you to be careful of the shadows, but I'm sure you already know that, too. That little friend of yours, the one with the necklace who came by when I visited last—you two were always getting a little too close to the shadows."

My heart beats a little faster. No one has mentioned Caris since the night we made the Purge, and somehow, Grandma has brought her memory to life. Then again, Grandma might only remember her because she's in Arizona. The fae's glamour could have skipped over her.

"I see things, Grandma," I say. "All the time."

Grandma clears her throat. "There was that trouble with you in middle school. I hoped you would figure things out on your own. There's a whole world of dark things, Ashly. What I know for sure is that it's bad luck to talk about those things, or else you invite them closer. Then again, it's up to you whether to turn a blind eye or face the shadows straight on. Make your ancestors proud. Take care and be careful, dear."

"I will," I say.

When the line goes quiet, my heart sinks. There was so much more I wanted to ask. Whether Grandma can see as I see, she seems unwilling to say. Yet I hold on to hope that I'm not the only one. If the faeries are real, then of course I'm not the only one who can see them.

After a minute, Mom comes back for her phone. "How is Grandma?" she asks. "She was worried about you, you know?"

"I'm sorry," I say. "I made you all worried."

Mom settles onto the bed beside me. "It's not your fault that someone was out to get you and Jasmine. Bad things happen to good people. You're strong, though. You made it out of the woods on your own. You've always been that way. There's nothing you can't do when you set your mind on something."

Then it's time for me to make my mind up on what comes next for me. I could wait for Caris forever. I could follow Mom and Dad to Arizona. Or I can stop and face the shadows straight on.

"I don't think I should go to Arizona," I say. "I'm going to look for a job. Maybe there's a house where I can rent out a room. There are options for community college, too. I want to try to find my own way."

I may not have a solid plan yet, but I can take steps forward. Even if my last meeting with Caris was a dream, what she said was true. I bested an Unseelie all by myself. If I can do that, then I can take my own future by the reins.

Mom nods slowly. "You're young, and you always have

me and your dad. It's okay to take some risks. Just know that if you wind up in any trouble, we're a phone call and a plane ride away. No matter what. Whatever you choose, we want you to be happy."

"Thanks, Mom."

She plants a kiss on my forehead, and I don't push her off. I close my eyes and wish for a future where I belong. Even if that place doesn't exist yet, I can find it. I can carve out my own path. One mistake at a time.

❖

Late that night, I crack open my laptop and type my name onto a document. My government textbook yawns open beside me. I can't make heads or tails out of the Supreme Court decision that I'm supposed to write an analysis on. Once I finally locate the page that explains the purpose of the court appeal, a knock hits my bedroom door.

I jump in surprise, which is a punch to the stomach. I really need to be careful not to open the wound again. I won't be playing backyard tennis for a couple more months, at least. That gives me plenty of time to get my act together and graduate. If I don't go stir-crazy before then.

"What is it?" I call out.

The door creaks open. A leather boot steps in, followed by the faerie I know best. Caris glances over the purple lamps, the computer in my lap, the simple humanness of my room. When her dark eyes finally rest on me, I get swept up between a flurry of nerves and the desire to hold her.

"You've got iron on the floor beneath the window," she says.

"It's supposed to keep the faeries out."

She crouches down beside me and shuts my laptop. "Where we're going, there will be faeries everywhere. I've come to escort you to the Court of Farrow Wood."

"As in right now?" I'm wearing sweatpants and a cropped T-shirt. Compared to Caris's leather boots and black tunic, I'm underdressed for the faerie kingdom.

She smiles and helps me up by the hand. Even once I'm standing, she doesn't let go. "Right now," she says.

The promise she made to me led her back. I think about all my doubts, my impatience. Caris has always been with me, and she always will.

There is a future out there for me, in a world where I belong, where I'm no longer *out of touch with reality*. With the fae, I'll be a human girl with the Sight, nothing more or less. Maybe now I can discover joys and terrors unlike anything I've experienced before.

Even though I've never fit in at school or home or tennis, there is a comfort in what I already know. I've figured out how to fake my way through the day. Once I follow Caris out the door, I'll no longer be able to hide. But I'm ready for whatever comes next. Now that the fighting and danger have passed, I'm no longer afraid of the forests of the night.

I grab Caris's jean jacket and lace on a pair of sneakers. "What about my parents? I never said good-bye."

She smiles. "You did, or so they'll remember."

"Will I ever see them again?"

"You can travel back and forth, as I have. You won't be a prisoner of Farrow Wood. But you might discover that you won't want to come back."

With a deep breath, I cross into the hallway. We slip past my parents' bedroom, and I silently promise them that I'll return soon, that I won't be gone forever, that I'll never forget them.

Then I keep going, so I won't second-guess myself into staying stagnant.

Our footfalls are the only sound as we reach the door and step into the night. There's a dark horse on the lawn. Its phosphorescent eyes bore into us, bewitching and restless.

"If you're polite, the Phooka will give us a ride," Caris says while petting the horse that must really be a faerie. "It's a long way to the Court of Farrow Wood."

"Yeah, right. Like I've ever ridden a horse."

Caris slips her boot into a stirrup and jumps onto the Phooka's back. "Are you scared, then?"

"I'm pretty sure my doctors wouldn't approve of any horseback riding."

She shakes her head. "Not of the horse. Where we're going, you'll no longer be the only one who sees the world for what it is. Let go of your fear."

All my life I've been resisting what no one else could see right in front of them. I've been screaming to be believed, and I've been pressured into silence. I've shouldered shame for the sake of others' comfort. In the Court of Farrow Wood, there will be no more hiding. I'll be free to laugh and to cry, to speak and to fight without masking all the reasons why. My gifts will be known, and my faults will be mine. What might it be like to no longer burn myself out?

Caris reaches out a hand. I fit my foot into the stirrup, and she guides me up so smoothly that there's no pain. I glide into the saddle with my back against her chest. My home, the street, and the night look completely different from up here. The stars blaze in the sky, vast and inviting. Nothing will ever be the same again.

"What's scary is that I'm about to find out for sure if the fae are real," I say. "It all depends on whether or not I wake up in my room in a bit."

Caris leans her cheek against mine, and I can feel her smile against my skin. I lean into that smile.

"Let me know if it's real in the morning," she says. "For now, it's time to move."

ACKNOWLEDGMENTS

As a child, I used to roam through fields and copses of trees, hoping to find faeries. I never found one, but I do see things that other people don't see. I am Autistic, and I have sensory processing differences. Because of these differences, I often hear and see little details that other people glance over. In school, I would talk about all these details, but my peers laughed at me or called me weird. I was often teased for my strong reactions to what others saw as small pieces of a bigger picture. As such, I personally want to thank the few school friends I had who never laughed at my differences. To Casey Klein, thank you for always seeking magic alongside me. To Chelsea Sanchez, I am eternally grateful for your high school friendship; changing schools during my senior year was a terrifying experience, but our excursions through nature and at the beach made all the difference. To Arianna Guerrero, our friendship in middle school and high school, filled with strange conversations about the bizarre and a love for the dark and magical, was and continues to be an anchor for me.

I also want to thank the people in my life who embrace my differences and see the beauty that unfolds when a person processes sensory input in a unique way. You know who you are. And lastly, to Bridget Degnan, my partner and most avid reader, thank you for your never-ending support. My stories would still be locked up in my mind if you didn't beg me to share them with you.

About the Author

Lauren Melissa Ellzey—known as @autienelle on Instagram—is a Black multiracial, queer, and Autistic author and activist. Her work has crossed paths with disability justice platforms such as NeuroClastic, AbleZine, and Cripple Media. She completed her BA at Scripps College, where she received the Crombie Allen Award for creative writing, and her MS in library and information science at Syracuse University. Lauren Melissa lives and works in New York City.

Young Adult Titles From Bold Strokes Books

Gimmicks and Glamour by Lauren Melissa Ellzey. Ashly has learned to hide her Sight, but as she speeds toward high school graduation she must protect the classmates she claims to hate from an evil that no one else sees. (978-1-63679-401-3)

A Talent Within by Suzanne Lenoir. Evelyne, born into nobility, and Annika, a peasant girl with a deadly secret, struggle to change their destinies in Valmora, a medieval world controlled by religion, magic, and men. (978-1-63679-423-5)

Take Her Down by Lauren Emily Whalen. Stakes are cutthroat, scheming is creative, and loyalty is ever-changing in this queer, female-driven YA retelling of Shakespeare's *Julius Caesar*. (978-1-63679-089-3)

Two Winters by Lauren Emily Whalen. A modern YA retelling of Shakespeare's *The Winter's Tale* about birth, death, Catholic school, improv comedy, and the healing nature of time. (978-1-63679-019-0)

Boy at the Window by Lauren Melissa Ellzey. Daniel Kim struggles to hold onto reality while haunted by both his very-present past and his never-present parents. Jiwon Yoon may be the only one who can break Daniel free. (978-1-63679-092-3)

Three Left Turns to Nowhere by Jeffrey Ricker, J. Marshall Freeman & 'Nathan Burgoine. Three strangers heading to a convention in Toronto are stranded in rural Ontario, where a small town with a subtle kind of magic leads each to discover what he's been searching for. (978-1-63679-050-3)

#shedeservedit by Greg Herren. When his gay best friend, and high school football star, is murdered, Alex Wheeler is a suspect and must find the truth to clear himself. (978-1-63555-996-5)

The Infinite Summer by Morgan Lee Miller. While spending the summer with her dad in a small beach town, Remi Brenner falls for Harper Hebert and accidentally finds herself tangled up in an intense restaurant rivalry between her famous stepmom and her first love. (978-1-63555-969-9)

Bury Me in Shadows by Greg Herren. College student Jake Chapman is forced to spend the summer at his dying grandmother's home and soon finds danger from long-buried family secrets. (978-1-63555-993-4)

I Am Chris by R Kent. There's one saving grace to losing everything and moving away. Nobody knows her as Chrissy Taylor. Now Chris can live who he truly is. (978-1-63555-904-0)

The Dubious Gift of Dragon Blood by J. Marshall Freeman. One day Crispin is a lonely high school student—the next he is fighting a war in a land ruled by dragons, his otherworldly boyfriend at his side. (978-1-63555-725-1)

Jellicle Girl by Stevie Mikayne. One dark summer night, Beth and Jackie go out to the canoe dock. Two years later, Beth is still carrying the weight of what happened to Jackie. (978-1-63555-691-9)

All the Worlds Between Us by Morgan Lee Miller. High school senior Quinn Hughes discovers that a broken friendship is actually a door propped open for an unexpected romance. (978-1-63555-457-1)

Exit Plans for Teenage Freaks by 'Nathan Burgoine. Cole always has a plan—especially for escaping his small-town reputation as "that kid who was kidnapped when he was four"—but when he teleports to a museum, it's time to face facts: it's possible he's a total freak after all. (978-1-163555-098-6)

Rocks and Stars by Sam Ledel. Kyle's struggle to own who she is and what she really wants may end up landing her on the bench and without the woman of her dreams. (978-1-63555-156-3)